Evil Streak

Evil Streak

Peter Conway

ROBERT HALE · LONDON

© Peter Conway 2006
First published in Great Britain 2006

ISBN-10: 0-7090-8058-1
ISBN-13: 978-0-7090-8058-9

Robert Hale Limited
Clerkenwell House
Clerkenwell Green
London EC1R 0HT

The right of Peter Conway to be identified as author of this work
has been asserted by him in accordance with the Copyright,
Designs and Patents Act 1988

2 4 6 8 10 9 7 5 3 1

Typeset in 11/15pt Palatino
Printed in Great Britain by St Edmundsbury Press
Bury St Edmunds, Suffolk.
Bound by Woolnough Bookbinding Limited

CHAPTER ONE

'What's that you're working on, Phil?'

The young man, who had been tightening a clamp on a piece of scaffolding, jumped down to the ground.

'Oh, hello, Sir Geoffrey. It's part of the course for Mr Stringer's obstacle race.'

'Hmm, looks pretty formidable to me. Now don't go wearing yourself out, will you? I'm supposed to be impartial, but it's high time the South won the cricket and I happen to know that they're depending on you for a few wickets.'

Belling saw to his amusement that Phil Rouse, the son of his farm manager, wasn't really listening, being too occupied in looking at the girl, who was practising the high jump a few yards away. He didn't blame the young fellow. Linda Baines, the fifteen-year-old daughter of his chauffeur, was, unlike the others, in proper athletics kit with shorts so brief that when she bent down to adjust her spiked shoes they were treated to a tantalizing glimpse of the crease at the base of her trim backside. She wasn't wearing anything under her shirt, either, which became only too obvious when she jumped up a few times before beginning her run-up.

Belling shook his head. He wasn't thinking so much of

the girl as her mother. Rose had been one of the maids up at the mansion and he had been delighted when she married Baines, his chauffeur. He had let the newlyweds have the lodge and they had been so happy, particularly when Linda was born some eighteen months later. It was when the baby was a year old and had just taken her first faltering steps, that Rose had bent down to scoop her up just as she was about to fall and had felt a sudden shower of pins and needles shooting down the backs of her legs. That was the start of the multiple sclerosis that was to lead her becoming bed-bound, incontinent and totally dependent on her husband.

Belling was shaken from his reverie by the arrival of the groundsman.

'Wicket going to play well, Henry?'

'As well as it's ever done, sir.'

'You've done a grand job – the whole ground's looking an absolute picture.'

Indeed it was, Belling thought. The land, which had belonged to his family for generations, had originally been used for grazing and then, in the nineteen twenties, his father had had it made into a polo ground. With the coming of the war it had reverted to its old use, but afterwards, when the old man died and he came into the estate, Belling had the idea of converting it into a sports ground for the town and very popular it had proved, too. Funds had been raised locally to provide a proper pavilion and it had become a focus for leisure activities of all kinds.

On the late May public holiday what had started as a cricket match between those living north and south of the main street had developed into a day out for everyone. There were food and drink stalls, pony-rides, a coconut-

EVIL STREAK

shy, a variety of serious and not so serious athletic events and the long jump pit was given over to the toddlers.

'Looks like being a beautiful day, not like last year, eh Henry?'

The man laughed. 'Who could forget that?'

With fifteen of the forty overs of the North's innings still to go, the cricket match looked like petering out with an easy win for them. The critical point came when, after having dismissed the South for a hundred and fifty-seven, which did not look like being nearly enough, the North were sixty for one wicket off ten overs and were going strongly. It was then that Phil Rouse produced a ball that hit the seam, came back a long way from outside the off stump and bowled Ted Parsmore. Ted was easily the best batsman on either side, having played many times for Oxfordshire in the Minor Counties Championship and he had been the scourge of the South for a number of years.

'Well bowled, lad,' the man said, as he walked out. 'That one was far too good for me.'

Phil Rouse glowed with pleasure at all the praise, even his father managing a gruff 'well done, son', and with his confidence sky-high, he took a further quick couple of wickets. After that the runs dried up and, with the approaching tea-interval, a somnolent atmosphere pervaded the whole ground.

'God, I'm bored,' Linda said to her friend as they sat on the edge of the boundary line. 'Why don't we leave?'

Tracey looked across at her. 'You could always liven things up a bit.'

'Just tell me how.'

'Well, you could ... but then you'd never dare.'

'Who says? What wouldn't I dare?'

'To do a streak.'

Colour had suddenly come into Linda's cheeks, but Tracey knew her friend well enough to know that it was a flush of excitement, not embarrassment.

'What would you give me if I do?'

Tracey thought for a moment; it was her birthday soon and she was sure she could persuade her uncle to give her another one.

'You could have my iPod, but you'd have to do it properly, everything off, the lot, and you'd have to go right across the ground.'

Linda bit her lip for a moment and then nodded. 'All right, but I can't undress here – someone would stop me.'

'You could go behind that tree.'

Even when her friend got up Tracey didn't really believe that she was going to do it. Topless, perhaps, but surely not the whole lot. In the event the streak exceeded her wildest expectations. The girl, the white areas on her body which had been protected from the sun by her bikini accentuating her nakedness, trotted out from behind the tree and on to the field. It would have created enough of a sensation if she had just continued on her way across to the other side, but she didn't. She stopped in front of Cyril Atherton, the vicar, who was umpiring at one end, slowly turned her back on him and then did a perfect handstand, holding the position for a full ten seconds before coming down, facing him again and curtsying.

For what seemed an age no one moved, then pandemonium broke loose. There was a mixture of booing, cheering and clapping from the spectators, Sir Geoffrey, who was umpiring at square leg, hurried across to restrain the vicar, who had pulled out one of the stumps and seemed intent on doing Linda a serious injury with it and Sergeant Bert

Stringer ran on to the field, put his coat around the girl's shoulders and hustled her into the pavilion, studiously avoiding the stares and grins of those occupying the deckchairs in front of it.

Sir Geoffrey managed to get the game going again somehow and no one took any notice of Tracey as she walked round the ground behind the spectators and slipped into the pavilion by the back entrance, where she found Bert Stringer pacing around in front of the shower room, in which he had obviously put her friend.

'And what do you want?' he said to her brusquely.

'I've got Linda's clothes here.'

'Oh you have, have you?'

Bert Stringer would have liked nothing better than to have wiped the sly grin off her face with the back of his hand, but the days when he could have done that and got away with it were long past, as he very well knew and regretted.

'And you had nothing to do with that little exhibition, I suppose?'

'Me, Mr Stringer?'

'Yes, you. You get a big kick out of persuading Linda to do all the things you haven't the cheek or the guts to do yourself, don't you?'

'I don't know what you're talking about!'

'One of these days you're going to go too far and I'm warning you, young lady, I've got my eye on you. Now get out of my sight before I lose my temper.'

It was a hot June afternoon, a few weeks after the events on the cricket field, and George Baines had been stuck on the same paragraph of the account of the previous day's play in the test match in the Sunday paper for five minutes.

Eventually, after his head had dropped forward for the third time, he gave up the struggle and leaned back in the armchair, surrendering to sleep. When he began to snore gently the girl in jeans, white shirt and red cardigan, who was sitting at the table by the window on the other side of the room, glanced round and very carefully put down the plastic ruler and her pencil, then eased her chair back and stood up. She waited there motionless until she was quite sure that her father was properly asleep, then tiptoed across the carpet and up the stairs, which led directly out of the living-room, avoiding the creaking step. The door of her parents' bedroom was open, but her mother was lying on her side with her back to the door and didn't move as she crept across the landing and into the bathroom.

Ten minutes later she was ready and, with the same care, went back down the stairs, turned the handle of the front door and pulled. When it failed to move, she tried again, this time harder, and it suddenly came open, giving a loud squeak. Instantly George Baines was awake, jerking upright and looking round.

'Where do you think you're orf to?'

'Just going to see Tracey.'

'What abaht yer homework?'

'I'll finish it when I get back.'

'That's what you said yesterday.' He glanced at the clock on the mantelpiece and saw that it was just after three o'clock. 'You're to be back not a minute after five – do you 'ear me?'

'Don't worry, Dad.'

'I do worry, Linda. Your school work's not going well an' you know what Miss Pembleton said an' ...'

''Bye, Dad.'

'Linda!'

Anger flared briefly inside him and he got to his feet, taking a pace towards his daughter, but by the time he was half-way across the room she had slipped through the door and shut it behind her. He made a half-hearted attempt to run after her, but he was still feeling light-headed after his sudden awakening. He stopped, standing by the door, then went slowly up the stairs as he heard the sound from the floor above.

'Wot is it, love?'

He had no need to ask; Rose had slipped sideways off her pillows and was making feeble efforts to get herself back. With practised skill Baines rolled her over, checked that there were no red marks on her skin, smoothed down the undersheet and, after ensuring that the catheter wasn't pulling uncomfortably, turned her so that she was lying on her back.

'Does that feel better?'

He regretted the question as soon as he had asked it, her attempt at a reply merely producing a series of unco-ordinated grunts and a violent, uncontrollable shaking of her head and arms. By gently pressing on her forehead with his hand he managed to steady her sufficiently to allow her to take a few sips of lemon barley water, then he drew the chair up by the side of the bed, taking her hand in his.

'I'll sit wiv you for a bit, if you like, Rose. Linda's just gone aht to see Tracey; I've lost another battle over 'er 'omework, but she promised to be back by five.'

Linda hadn't, of course, promised any such thing, but he wasn't going to tell Rose that. She responded, as she always did, by giving him a gentle squeeze with her fingers, but even that was sufficient to set her arms and head into violent motion again. Baines had spent so many hours with her, particularly over the previous two years, ever since she had been confined, at first to her wheelchair and then to bed, that he was sensitive to the least change in her condition. Something else had gone wrong with the faltering and stricken mechanism that was her nervous system – he was sure of it. It wasn't only that her tremor was so much worse, there was also something seriously amiss with her breathing; already in the short time that he had been sitting by the bed, there had been a couple of periods lasting twenty to thirty seconds during which her chest hadn't moved at all.

When the rhythm picked up again and he watched the steady rise and fall of her chest, he suddenly had an almost irresistible impulse to pick up one of the pillows and press it over her mouth. Would it be so very wrong? He and Sir Geoffrey had had no difficulty recently in agreeing that it had been time to put down Blackie, the old labrador. He was thirteen, practically blind, in pain from arthritis, and when he became incontinent and went off his food it was clear that the poor old fellow had had enough. A visit from a sympathetic vet, a last wag of his tail as Sir Geoffrey cradled the animal's head, a quick injection and it was all over.

If everyone approved of giving an animal a humane and dignified end like that, why couldn't one do the same for human beings, particularly for those like Rose, whose multiple sclerosis was both incurable and had reduced her to her present pitiful state? What he was witnessing now was the very reverse of dignified; what point was there to life when she had a humiliating tube sticking into her, was unable to communicate, her eyes were jerking about and he had to anticipate her every need? Dr Crichton obviously felt the same way about it and hadn't treated her last chest infection, but she had got over that without antibiotics and so the misery had continued.

Baines had had to take so much time off that when Sir Geoffrey summoned him to his study he feared the worst, but he ought to have known better.

'George,' his employer had said, 'I know just how rough things have been and I think you have quite enough to do without trying to struggle on here at work as well. With all the DSS allowances and a small retainer from me you should be able to manage all right financially.'

'Retainer, Sir Geoffrey?'

'You didn't think you were going to escape me that easily, did you? Anyway, you know that I've never been able to cope with cars and I'll expect you to go on cleaning and maintaining the things; you'll be able to do that outside the lodge just as easily as you can up here.'

'You mean we'll be able to stay in the lodge?'

'The lodge is yours as long as you, Rose and Linda want to use it. It'll probably embarrass you, but I'd just like you to know that I think you've done a wonderful job in looking after Rose, and as to Linda, she's a credit to you both.'

That might have been true when Sir Geoffrey had said it, but that had been two years ago and it certainly wasn't true now. The happy small girl, who had enjoyed running errands for her mother, who helped with the housework and did simple bits of cooking, had grown six inches and become a sulky, pouting menace, who spent as much time out of the house as possible. She was just about prepared to help with the washing-up, but that was about the extent of it. About the only consolation was that she did keep herself and her clothes clean and looked after her own room; his own problems with laundry were solved by Sir Geoffrey who included it with that from the manor.

George Baines had been so worried about Linda that he

went up to the school to see Miss Pembleton, the one member of staff for whom she seemed to have any respect. The PE teacher promised to have a chat to her and although that improved things for a few days, it didn't last.

'Don't worry, Mr Baines,' the woman had said when he went up there again, 'lots of girls are difficult at her age – she'll be all right soon and adolescents are always worse at home than they are anywhere else. I'll keep a special eye on her for you.'

A fat lot of good that had done, he thought. Linda had become more and more secretive, taken to locking her bedroom door and hardly said a word to him. After he had seen a TV programme on teenage drug-taking he even wondered about that, but when he came to watch her more carefully he was at least reassured on that score. She was obviously glowing with health – anyone could see that. Her jet-black hair shone so that it almost glowed, her complexion was clear, she had an abundance of physical energy, athletics being the one thing on which she was really keen at school, and he couldn't complain about her appetite. If it hadn't been for her manner, her moods and rudeness, she would have been a very attractive girl. Physically, she *was* a very attractive girl and that was another worry.

Only two weeks earlier when Sir Geoffrey had taken her and Tracey to the local gymkhana, he had seen young Phil Rouse, one of the gardeners, looking at her as she climbed into the Jaguar. He was honest enough to admit to himself that he had given many a young woman looks like that when he had been a youngster and he wasn't above doing it still whenever the opportunity arose, which nowadays was almost never, but none of that made it any easier for him when the object of that attention was fifteen and his only child. They had had to wait so long for Linda and she had been such a delight to them both, but now.... He knew perfectly well that he wasn't being fair. Poor Linda! What she had needed was a mother, brothers and sisters and a father who didn't have to spend his whole time being a nursemaid. It wasn't her fault and perhaps, as Miss Pembleton had said, it would turn out all right in the long run. It wasn't until he was helping himself to a beer after he had watched on TV the cricket team he supported win off the third ball of the last over that he suddenly realized how late it was.

Rose had fallen asleep and he walked the few yards down the drive and stood looking up the road. Times had changed with a vengeance, he thought, not least because in his day of wartime food and rationing, girls of fifteen, or even older, were girls, not fully developed young women who wore skin-tight jeans and read articles about sex and other topics in perfectly respectable magazines, articles which at that time would have been the subject of prose-cutions and the magazines taken off the news-stands. No, things were very different now and he wasn't by any means sure that it was for the better. At least as a boy he hadn't been spoiled silly, nor had he and his brothers and sisters spent their whole time in front of the television.

When seven o'clock came he began to get really worried, particularly after he had telephoned Tracey's mother and discovered that her daughter had been out for a bicycle ride on her own all afternoon and hadn't seen Linda at all. If he were to ring the police, he knew that it would be all over the village inside twenty-four hours and yet.... He decided to turn Rose and then get in touch with Sir Geoffrey – he'd know what to do.

He had just finished rubbing Rose's back when he heard the knock on the front door. Looking through the window he saw the police Corsa standing outside. Even before he had opened the door and saw the expression on young Fred Grimes' face he knew that something terrible had happened.

'It's Linda. Something's 'appened to Linda, 'asn't it?' Grimes nodded, unable to meet his gaze. 'You'd better come in.'

CHAPTER TWO

Detective Chief Superintendent Bill Watson was fifty-three, a stocky, burly man, who had long since lost the battle against middle-age spread. With his ruddy complexion, the faint country burr in his voice and his strong hands with their roughened fingers, he looked like the farmers that both his father and brother were. He also had an avuncular aura about him, which had given him his nickname of 'Uncle Bill', and his being known as a family man with four children and for his interest and skill in carpentry, any number of people had been deceived into thinking that he was just too amiable and indeed too soft for his job.

They couldn't have been more wrong. Bill Watson was a tough, career policeman with thirty-three years' service behind him and an absolute dedication to his job. He was also capable of ferocious outbursts of temper, which were all the more terrifying for being on show only on very rare occasions. The last time had been when the case against Daniel Rivers had run into difficulties.

'Russell,' he had said to the inspector who had interviewed and taken statements from Kevin Whitestone, the key witness, 'do you think I've completely lost my marbles?'

'No, sir.'

Watson waved the piece of paper in the man's face. 'That boy Whitestone has an IQ in the middle seventies and would never say the things you've got written down here, and as for this ...' He lifted up the cassette. 'Even my grandmother, who's ninety-three and deaf as a post could tell that it's been edited.'

'But Rivers is guilty, sir. We all know he is.'

'Maybe he is, but the quickest way to let him get away with it is to fabricate evidence. Don't the Guildford Four, the Birmingham Six and the Tottenham Three mean anything to you at all, Russell? You're so fucking stupid I don't suppose you even realize that you'd be inside yourself and my head would be on the chopping-block if an even half-decent barrister got hold of this load of crap.'

Russell got to his feet and backed away as Watson began to rise from his chair, feeling the sweat trickling down the back of his neck as he saw the expression on the other man's face.

'Get out and consider this your lucky day. I expect to see your letter of resignation on my desk before the day is out.'

The Russell business had happened only four weeks earlier and on top of that there was now a murder to cope with.

'Murder?' Alan Burgess, Watson's number two, asked after he had been summoned to the office.

Watson nodded. 'I was called out late yesterday afternoon. A woman walking her dog found the body in the undergrowth off a country lane not far from Welbury. Do you know Welbury?'

Burgess shook his head. 'Only the name.'

'It's a smallish town, a dozen or so miles from Reading, just off the old Great West Road. Sleepy sort of place. Anyway, a fifteen-year-old girl by the name of Linda

Baines was found lying on her back on a carpet of leaves. I sent for Rawlings, but it was obvious what had happened; she was naked below the waist apart from her left sock and her legs were abducted to about forty-five degrees in the classical rape position. There was a nasty abrasion on the outer side of the lower part of her right leg and a severe injury to the left side of her head, which was probably the cause of her death.'

'How come she was identified so quickly?'

'The woman who found her recognized her as a local girl and her father made a formal identification later that evening.'

'Anything else found at the site?'

Watson pushed the pile of photographs across the desk. 'Some bits of orange plastic, which look as if they probably came from the trafficator cover of a car, some bloodstains on a large stone a few feet from the road and her bike, with its right pedal bent and scratched, lying quite close to her.'

'So it looks as if she was run down by a car, knocked out in the fall, then pulled into the undergrowth, raped and left to die.'

'That's about the size of it, but we should know for certain after the post-mortem, which is scheduled for tomorrow afternoon.'

'Are you going?'

'Yes and I'd like you to join me. By the way, I've decided to put Mark Sinclair on to the case. What do you think?'

'Sinclair?'

'You needn't sound so surprised. Yes, I know he looks and sounds like a stockbroker, but underneath all the veneer he's one of the ablest men we've got and he's just the bloke to cope with Belling.'

'Belling?'

'He's the employer of the murdered girl's father, the local squire and landowner and that's not all – he's a magistrate and also happens to be a personal friend of the chief constable.'

'Enough said, but you asked me what I thought and you might as well know that despite all that it won't do.'

'Why not?'

'Because the other DIs resent the bugger; he's not one of the boys, university and, even worse for these parts, Oxford University-educated, went shooting up the promotional ladder, a loner. Isn't that enough?'

'We need someone who's good at working on his own. I don't need to tell you that we're run off our feet with "Operation Speed" and I can't spare a whole team at the moment. It's bad enough having to find sufficient men to search that copse and as it is, you and I'll have to cope with the bloody media – we certainly can't delegate that, not in the present climate. There's one other reason why I think he's the best choice.'

'Oh, and what's that?'

'He knows how to handle Rawlings – that man gets on my wick.'

'Mine, too. I can see you've made up your mind, but don't say I didn't warn you.'

'What I've decided to do is to give him a run for his money and it's not as if he'll be entirely on his own. I've already put someone else on to those bits of broken plastic and we're running a computer check on any sex offenders in the area.'

'Have you told Sinclair yet?'

'He's due in ten minutes.'

'You won't be wanting me here, will you, Bill?'

'No, Alan, I won't. I don't want his confidence totally destroyed before he's even started.'

'I only wish I really had that effect on him – he always makes me feel like a new recruit.'

Mark Sinclair was sitting in the secretary's office and Burgess gave him a curt nod as he passed through. Just typical of the bugger to get up out of his chair, he thought. Smarmy bastard!

At that moment Watson was glancing at Sinclair's personal file. Although he didn't share Burgess's view of the man, he knew exactly why he was so unpopular; to get on with your colleagues in an organization like the police force, he thought, you needed to be a good deal more than hard-working, able and unfailingly polite to everyone. You needed to belong, to be part of the team, not to stick out from the others like a sore thumb and make them feel uncomfortable. That particular ability even seemed to affect Rawlings. The forensic pathologist liked nothing better than to embarrass the officers, particularly the women, with his abrasive manner and his coarse jokes, but he never tried it on with Sinclair, any more than Burgess would swear in front of him, which was saying something.

Public school, second-class honours in English at Oxford and in the university golf team for three years, one would have expected him to go into a merchant bank, or become a diplomat – what on earth had made him choose a career in the police force? He was thirty-one, lived alone in a small house in Oxford and, apart from golf, his interests outside work were listed as chess and the theatre. He was tall, slim and good-looking in a distinctly old-fashioned way with his neat haircut and immaculate suits. And why was he neither married, nor did he appear to have a girlfriend? Was he just uninterested in women, did he have someone hidden away, or was he gay? Perhaps that was the reason why the only people who seemed to like him were the young WPCs. Was that because they didn't feel threatened by him?

Watson put the file in a drawer in his desk and pressed the buzzer. 'I'll be leaving the preliminary enquiries to you,' he said to Sinclair when he had given him an outline of the case, 'and I can only spare you one person to help during the assessment period. Any ideas about whom you'd like?'

'You said that the wood is being searched today?'

'Yes. I don't expect them to find anything new, but you know how it is; the media expect it and we have to go through the motions. Fowler may just turn up something on those bits of plastic and you'll have the computer print-out of the sex offenders in the locality.'

Sinclair looked through the photographs and the reports of the pathologist and the scene-of-crime men.

'I think that one of the WPCs would be an advantage, particularly in handling the family in the early stages.'

'I agree. Got anyone particular in mind?'

'I'll have to think about it and see who's available.'

'Very well, but don't take too long about it. I'm going to the post-mortem with Mr Burgess tomorrow afternoon at one-thirty; although, ideally, I would have liked you to be there, Rawlings won't have more than two of us, but at least he has agreed to see you on Wednesday morning.'

'I'll come up with a name by first thing tomorrow.'

'All right.' He flicked over the page in his diary. 'Make it eight o'clock and bring her along with you.'

Fiona Campbell massaged her aching neck and looked out of the window to rest her eyes. Just her luck, she thought, to have had experience of word processors and computers and to be available when the usual operator was off sick. God, what a boring job!

'Miss Campbell!'

She gave a guilty start and looked round to see Inspector Sinclair standing at the door.

'Sorry to disturb you, but I'd like a word with you in my office.'

All the way up there she was wondering what she had done wrong. She was sitting nervously on the edge of the chair he had offered her when he gave her a smile.

'Don't look so worried; I was just wondering if you'd like to work with me on a case – it's the rape and murder of a girl near Welbury.'

Half an hour later Fiona was closing down the computer; in one way she was scarcely able to believe her good fortune in having the opportunity to get away from the wretched machine, but would she be able to cope, particularly with a case involving rape? There was only one way to find out and that was not by giving up before she had started.

'We'll be on our own to begin with,' Sinclair had said, 'and I'll be particularly looking for your help with her family and school – it's bound to be a very difficult time for all of them. At this stage there is, of course, no means of knowing how long the case is going to last, but it's certain to mean working long hours and very probably at weekends – that cause you any problems?'

'No, sir.'

'Good. I'll just have to check with Mr Watson that it's all right for you to be taken off your present job. He also wants to see you first thing in the morning, but I don't anticipate any difficulties. If he agrees we can have a further talk about it afterwards.'

Fiona was used to being told exactly what to do and when, not whether, she would like to, and, in her admittedly limited experience, she had found that the WPCs were usually given the sort of jobs that had the more feminist of her contemporaries constantly complaining.

'There's something fishy about this,' Sharon Morris said to her over a cup of tea in the canteen.

'What do you mean, fishy?'

'You getting given a decent job. If you ask me, that MCP Sinclair must fancy you. If I were you I'd buy a chastity belt with a combination lock on it.'

'Don't be daft. You know perfectly well that he's not like that; you were saying only the other day that he's the one male officer who doesn't either talk down or dirty to us.'

'That's why he's so dangerous. He's the crafty, sneaky type, who'll sweet-talk his way up under that kilt of yours.'

'Don't be so soft.'

'Don't say I didn't warn you.'

Sharon always talked like that, Fiona said to herself as she waited outside Sinclair's office the following morning, but ... but nothing. How was she going to gain experience if she started to have reservations about the first really decent opportunity that had come her way, even before she had started?

The meeting with the chief superintendent lasted only a matter of a few minutes, as he did little more than look her up and down and ask her a few questions about what she had been doing, before agreeing that she could be transferred to work on the murder inquiry.

'That's the first hurdle over,' Sinclair said when they were back in his office. 'Why not read the file now and then we can have a preliminary chat about it?'

The photographs were in sharp focus and utterly revealing in their detail, but when she thought about it later Fiona realized that the fact that he had given them to her almost casually and without comment did a great deal for her confidence. Brutal facts and sordid circumstances were all part of the job and if she couldn't cope with them she had no business to have gone into the police force in the first place and that was all there was to it.

'What's your first impression?' he asked when she had finished.

Fiona looked up and took a deep breath. 'I don't think there's enough to go on yet to have one – I'd like to hear the results of the post-mortem for one thing.'

'Good for you,' he said with a smile. 'The balance between useless speculation and the throwing out of ideas is a fine one and I agree with you that we need to know more. Ideally, I would have liked both of us to have attended the autopsy, but both Watson and Burgess are going and Rawlings won't accept anyone else. Anyway, he has agreed to see us at eight o'clock on Wednesday morning and that will give us a chance to question him, that is if we can get a word in edgeways. A word of warning about Rawlings: don't on any account let him upset you. Doctors and, in my experience, particularly forensic pathologists, have a curious sense of humour – they tend to make jokes about things that most people don't find in the least funny and even upsetting. Having said that, we are not exactly guiltless in that regard – I suppose it must help to keep us sane. The point is that Rawlings enjoys having a go at us and the greater the reaction, the more pleasure he gets out of it. Amongst other things, he seems to think that women, with the notable exception of that gorgon of a secretary of his, Miss Ryle, aren't psychologically robust enough for police work and to prove the point he likes to twist the knife in anyone brave or foolhardy enough to run the gauntlet. You've been in court a few times, haven't you?'

'Yes.'

'And what would you say was the best way to cope with a tricky coroner or an aggressive barrister?'

'Do your homework, stick to the facts, don't say too much and keep your cool.'

'That's exactly the right way to deal with Rawlings, too, which means that some homework on rape is required. I can lend you some books and, most important, a reprint of an article by Rawlings. I would suggest that you read them now and we can go over some of the points this afternoon.'

'How did you get on?' Sinclair asked the following day.

'Well enough to realize how little I knew about it and I'm not sure how much wiser I am now. I feel fairly confident about the forensic bits and Dr Rawlings's special interest, but not with the psychological side.'

'That's not surprising. There are almost as many views about that subject as there are writers on it; there is even a difference of opinion about definition. Some people even include under rape, a wife or partner being pressured into having intercourse when they just don't happen to feel like it on a particular occasion. However, there are some pretty solid facts. Male on female is the most common type, but male on male, female on female and female on male all occur and in the majority of cases the rapist is known to the victim. Some rapists only ever attack particular classes of people such as children, prostitutes and even the elderly. Some feminist writers say that all men are potential rapists – the more extreme leave out the word "potential" – and it occurs worldwide, not seeming to be a cultural phenomenon. For years the work of Margaret Mead, an American anthropologist, suggested that rape did not occur in some cultures such as that in Samoa, but it appears that she was seriously misled and was wrong.'

'It says in one of the chapters I read that the sexual impulse in males and females is almost identical and that any differences are culturally determined. I find that very difficult to believe.'

'So do I. The importance of cultural factors in many forms of human behaviour has had a great vogue in recent years, largely because it leads sociologists to believe that if you alter the environment many problems will just melt away. In my view most of the evidence points in the other direction. As far as the sexual impulse is concerned, males have a different balance of hormones from females, they have different chromosomes and there are even slight but definite differences in the gross structure of their brains. They are, by and large, a great deal more aggressive, the sexual impulse is more easily aroused and correspondingly more difficult to resist. I know that many feminists pour scorn on that idea, but women are not immune from self-destructive impulses – anorexia nervosa is an example – and what could be more difficult to comprehend than an adolescent starving herself to death? Major differences in the sexual impulse between males and females can also be seen throughout the animal kingdom and I never did believe the statement that "man is not an animal". He is, and a most aggressive and dangerous one at that.'

'What about murder and rape?'

'You tell me.'

'Well, obviously if the victim fights back and screams, killing might be part of the general violence, the rapist could be a sadistic killer as well and, I suppose, just occasionally, death might be accidental, by that I mean that there was no intent and the force used was just too much, particularly if the victim was frail and elderly.'

'Well done. That just about covers it except for those cases in which the rapist realizes that his victim will be able to identify him and he kills to save himself from detection. Now, how about a session on Rawlings's pet hobby-horse? I haven't read it for some time and need to be reminded of it.'

'Enter!'

The shouted command came from behind the door of Dr Rawlings's office in response to Mark Sinclair's knock.

'Ah, Sinclair, good-morning.' The man behind the desk peered intently at Fiona over the top of his half-moon spectacles. 'And what have we here?'

'May I introduce DC Fiona Campbell, who is going to help me with this inquiry?'

'Is she, is she indeed? And what is this fresh-faced Scottish girl, or should I say lassie, which I take it that she is with a name like that, doing getting mixed up in such murky doings as murder and rape?'

'I'm trying to get as much and as broad an experience as I can and Inspector Sinclair has asked me to assist him,' Fiona said, giving the man a bright smile and ignoring his excruciating attempt at a Scottish accent.

'Hmm. Well at least you don't seem to mind being called a girl; I tried that one out on one of the female medical students the other day and received a regular ear-bashing. Sexist, patronizing, demeaning – quite an array of adjectives she produced – and all for an inoffensive little four-letter word! Now, I suppose you want to hear about this unfortunate young woman, Linda Baines?'

'We would indeed,' Sinclair said, looking, Fiona thought, totally at ease.

'Very well.' Rawlings replied, then without any warning at all he let out a stentorian bellow. 'Miss Ryle!'

Rawlings's secretary, who appeared at the door, might have looked frail, being painfully thin and with wispy, grey hair, but she was clearly made of stern stuff.

'There's no need to shout like that, Dr Rawlings. I'm not deaf, you know, and it embarrasses people.'

The forensic pathologist held up his hand imperiously to silence her. 'Three coffees, if you please, Miss Ryle, and don't try to slip in any of that decaffeinated muck – it inhibits the thought processes.'

'But your palpitations, Dr Rawlings; you know what the cardiologist said.'

'"Steady of heart and stout of hand", is that what you'd like me to be, Miss Ryle?'

'Yes, sir, and you most certainly won't be if you go on drinking strong coffee.'

'Pah! Do you know what else the cardiologist said?'

'No, sir.'

'The one piece of sense he uttered; he made it very clear that being thwarted was extremely bad for me. The coffee, if you'd be so kind, Miss Ryle, and some of your mother's excellent shortbread – Miss Campbell here is looking distinctly peckish having, unlike you, a healthy appetite and having missed out on her porridge and oat-cakes this morning due to the earliness of the hour. Oh, and Miss Ryle, the Baines' file if you'd be so kind.'

'It's on the chair by your desk, sir.'

Although he could easily have reached it without

getting up he snapped his fingers. When the woman ignored him and left the room he looked pointedly at Fiona, who picked it up and put it into his hand, giving him the merest suspicion of a smile.

After he had taken it Rawlings sat there for a moment, pressing his lips tightly together, his face getting a progressively deeper shade of red, then he hastily grabbed his handkerchief and began to splutter. Fiona took one anxious look towards Sinclair and when he failed to react, put her hand on the pathologist's shaking shoulder.

'Are you feeling all right, Dr Rawlings?'

The man wiped his streaming eyes and looked up at her.

'All right? Of course I'm all right; I just happened to remember the title of the poem from which that quotation came and was fool enough to associate it with Miss Ryle.' He gathered himself together with an enormous effort and stared at her for a moment. 'I take it that you've heard of DNA,' he rasped suddenly without any warning.

'Yes, I have,' Fiona replied, 'but I don't know much more about it than its name, deoxyribonucleic acid, that it's in two strands forming a double helix and that the pattern for every individual is distinct.'

'And where did you obtain those interesting pieces of information?'

'In the first place, from a TV programme on Crick and Watson and then I read your article on its use in forensic pathology.'

'Did you, did you indeed? Wonders will never cease. Well, at least you've remembered the name correctly and even that's more than a great many people, including the less enlightened members of my own profession, can muster. Care to learn a bit more?'

'Yes, I would.'

'DNA has been called "the molecule of life" because, as you rightly said, it has a double-stranded structure, which has the ability to split along its long axis. Each half is used as a template, or pattern, for the production of another molecule, which is the fundamental step in cell division.'

'And identification of people from body fluids is possible because each individual's DNA can now be analysed?'

'Fundamentally, that's true, but the process concerned with that analysis is far from simple. Bacterial enzymes are used to cut the DNA into fragments and it is this set of fragments that is specific to an individual. Until recently the process has been both cumbersome and tedious, but a new technique using PCR – polymerase chain reaction – has made it both simpler and quicker. Furthermore, very small quantities of blood and even a mouthwash or a single hair will produce sufficient cells to permit analysis. Here, you might like to study the latest paper I've just written on the subject; it's been my aim to eliminate the jargon as much as possible and you should be able to follow it.'

Fiona took the reprint from him. 'Thank you very much.'

'And you were able to get a specimen from the raped girl?' Sinclair asked.

'I did get some material from her all right, but she wasn't raped.'

'What? But what about these photographs that were taken at the scene of the crime?'

Sinclair took them out of the folder and laid them on Rawlings's desk.

'If my interpretation of the findings is correct, she was positioned to make it look like rape. You see, her knickers were … No, that's not the right word, what do you call those things these days, my dear?'

'Panties.'

'Hmm! Sounds distinctly twee to me, but one must keep up to date. What it is to have someone here *au courant* with the latest terminology! Miss Ryle is no help at all; all she could come up with was step-ins and even I know that that inelegant term went out with the Ark. I digress. Anyway, her panties,' he said, stressing the word very deliberately, 'had seminal stains on the inner aspect of the reinforced bit.' He snapped his fingers and looked at Fiona interrogatively.

'The gusset, sir.'

'I thought you were the lexical expert, Sinclair; I shall have to look to my laurels now with the two of you to correct me. Now, as you no doubt saw from the pictures, the body was found divested of both jeans and panties and what does that suggest to you, Miss Campbell?'

'That she had had intercourse earlier on.'

'Exactly. Further evidence was that there was no injury at all to the genital region, not even bruising.'

'I see,' said Sinclair, 'but you're not going to tell me that she wasn't murdered, either.'

'No. She was killed by a single blow to the left side of her head delivered with considerable force – her skull was fractured and what proved fatal was the massive haemorrhage affecting the underlying brain. Some of these haemorrhages take some time to accumulate, so it's possible that she didn't die immediately following the injury. At first sight it might have appeared that she had hit the stone with her head when catapulted off her bicycle, but in my opinion it was lifted and used as a club.'

'What makes you think that?'

'There was some blood on its under surface, which could not possibly have got there as the result of her fall.'

'Were you able to estimate the time of death?'

'It was a fine, dry, warm afternoon and as the result of body temperature measurement, I would say it was within two hours or so of my arrival on the scene, which was a few minutes after seven pm.'

'Did you find any other injuries?'

'Her right fibula was fractured in the region of that abrasion you no doubt saw in the photograph. Any other queries?'

'Not at present, thank you.'

'Miss Campbell?'

'Were you able to estimate the time of intercourse?'

Rawlings looked up in surprise. It was a rare experience for him to be confronted by a young woman who not only didn't appear to be in the least scared of him, but also asked intelligent questions. Before he had time to reply there was a knock on the door and his secretary put her head round it.

'What is it, Miss Ryle? Can't you see that I'm busy?'

'It's Dr Gardner, sir. He has an appointment at nine o'clock.'

'Tell him to wait.'

The pathologist had made no attempt at all to lower his voice and gave one of his vulpine grins as he saw the woman glance over her shoulder.

'Where was I? Ah yes, the time of the intercourse. Earlier that afternoon, I would say; I found mobile sperm when I took a vaginal specimen during my initial examination at the scene of the crime. That wasn't the only place I looked, either; would you care to hazard a guess as to where else, Miss Campbell?'

'The rectum.'

'And what makes you think that?'

'Because it's not uncommon for anal rape to occur at the same time as vaginal.'

'My goodness, Sinclair, you have found a veritable paragon. You're quite right, Miss Campbell, but on this occasion the anus was quite undamaged.'

'And you were able to do the DNA testing?'

'It has not yet been completed, but other material you may get from suspects would be gratefully received, not of course that I'm suggesting that you should take specimens from all the men in the area, which was done in Leicestershire a few years back – we do not have the resources for that.'

He got up from his chair and came to the door with them, much to the astonishment of his secretary who was left standing just inside her office, eyebrows raised in surprise.

'Do you think, Miss Ryle,' he said heavily, 'that you might be able to take a rest from doing your celebrated imitation of Lot's wife for long enough to show Dr Gardner in?'

CHAPTER THREE

'What did you make of all that?' Sinclair asked as they drove away from the hospital.

'It seems certain that Linda Baines was knocked off her bike by a car, which would explain the damage to the pedal and her fractured fibula, and was then killed by a blow on the head from that stone, but why should a simulated rape have been set up? I can't see any reason for the murderer to have done that.'

'Neither, for the moment, can I.'

'Were any fingerprints found on that stone?'

'Unfortunately not, nor on the fragments of the trafficator cover and only Linda's were on the bike. Why don't we go down to Welbury now and get a feel of the place? As a start, I suppose we ought to see Linda's parents, which is not a task I'm exactly looking forward to. I gather that the girl's father works for a local landowner, one Sir Geoffrey Belling, who is someone we'll have to handle with a certain amount of care – he's a friend of the chief constable. Evidently the two of them were together on some inquiry in Belfast to do with allegations against prison officers a few years ago and that's how they got to know one another. Would you be navigator? I've marked Welbury Hall on the map.'

The entrance to the drive of the Hall was guarded by some impressive-looking wrought-iron gates, which were open. Sinclair drove in and pulled up outside the lodge.

'It doesn't look very promising to me.' he said after there was no response to his ring. 'All the windows are shut as well.'

'Shall I take a look round the back?'

'Good idea.'

Fiona pushed her way through a tangle of brambles at the side of the house and was just trying the back door when she heard a sound behind her that sent a cold shiver right down the back of her spine. She whirled round to see the Alsatian advancing slowly towards her, growling menacingly.

'Can I help you?'

The elderly man, who was wearing a tweed suit and a matching deerstalker hat and who had come through the gate at the side of the garden behind the lodge, snapped his fingers and the dog moved to his side and sat down.

'Yes, we're looking for Mr and Mrs Baines.'

'If you're from the press, I've got no comment to make, no comment at all and I must ask you to leave.'

Fiona was just about to explain when Mark Sinclair appeared round the side of the house.

'Sir Geoffrey Belling? My name is Sinclair, Inspector Sinclair, and this is my assistant, Fiona Campbell.'

'Ah, yes. Daintree told me to expect you.' He shook their hands and stroked his chin with his hand. 'So you haven't heard?'

'Heard what?'

'Rose Baines died yesterday and George is staying with me at the moment. As you may imagine, what with

Linda's murder and now this, he's had more than he can take and he's under sedation.'

'So we won't be able to see him?'

'Certainly not today, I'm afraid, but why not come up to the Hall and I'll try to fill you in with some background.'

He led them up the drive, in through the large double doors at the front and into the study to the left of the hall.

'I don't normally believe in talking about people's personal lives behind their backs, but if you don't know about the severe stress that George has been under, you would, I'm quite sure, find it very difficult to know how best to handle the poor man.' He paused, flicked a cigarette half out of the packet he had taken from his pocket and after offering it to each of them in turn, lit it when they both refused. 'The first time I met George Baines was when he was up on a charge in front of me when he was doing his National Service in the army. One of the regular corporals had been bullying some of the new recruits – I won't bore you with the details, suffice it to say that it involved humiliating initiation ceremonies with sexual overtones – and George stood up to him. The corporal made the mistake of hitting George and you didn't hit streetwise Lambeth boys in those days and expect them not to retaliate.

'Anyway, I found out the truth of the matter and although he had any number of rough edges, I took to George Baines. He was straightforward, he was honest and he was plucky. To cut a long story short, he became my batman and when I retired a year or two later to look after this estate after my father died, he came to work for me here. George has always done anything, whatever I have asked him, willingly and efficiently and he's been with me ever since. He's a good mechanic, an excellent driver and can turn his hand to most things.

'I was delighted when he married Rose, who was one of the house servants. George is the salt of the earth, but he does have his moods and, at times, a blazing temper, and Rose was just what he needed. She was sweet-natured, fun and stopped him from taking life too seriously. They were so happy, particularly when, after a long wait, Linda was born and under the circumstances the multiple sclerosis that she contracted soon after, was especially cruel. Rose never complained, but it must have been torture for George to see her slowly being destroyed in front of his eyes. He was wonderful with her, quite exceptional, and I don't know how he stood it, particularly over the last two or three years. A big extra problem was Linda. She was the ideal child for them to start with, pretty and well-behaved, but at about the age of twelve, just when Rose was beginning to spend most of her time in a wheelchair, it all changed. She became petulant and rude and, on top of that, not long after, sexually provocative as well.'

'In what way?'

'Well, for one thing, it was the way she dressed. If Rose had been in better health, I'm quite sure she would have bought her clothes either for her or with her and would never have let her leave the house in skirts so short that they were positively indecent, or trousers so tight that one could see every detail of her anatomy. It wasn't only that, either, there was her manner. It's difficult to describe; it was something you had to see, or, dare I say it, experience.'

'She tried it on you, then?'

'Yes, even me, at my age, for God's sake. I used to let her exercise my hunters and one day after she had been thrown attempting a jump, I saw her beat the horse, whose fault it most certainly wasn't, with her riding crop. When she came in, I told her that if I ever saw her doing that again, not only would she never ride one of my horses again, but I'd give her a taste of her own medicine. It was a stupid thing for me to have said and she knew it; she pulled down her breeches and pants and bent over, looking at me over her shoulder with a wicked grin and said: "you can now, if you like. I won't tell anyone".' Belling shook his head. 'Little minx!'

'Do you suppose she was sexually promiscuous?'

'Was she just a daredevil or something more than that? I just don't know. Anyway, I'm the wrong person to ask; you could write a very large book about what I don't know about adolescent girls.'

'What about school?'

'She went to the local comprehensive here in Welbury; it not only serves the town, but also the villages in the vicinity and is an excellent place, even though I say it myself – I'm chairman of the board and the local parents take a lot of interest in it.'

'Did Linda have any special friends?'

'Yes, her best friend was Tracey Farrell, who is the daughter of my head gardener. I could never understand it – they were as different as chalk from cheese. They were both the same age, but Linda was a woman and Tracey is still a child. Linda wasn't interested in academic work and loved physical things such as riding, swimming and athletics, whereas Tracey is clumsy and, in all honesty, not all that good at anything. The same thing was true about their looks; Tracey is rather a plain girl, whereas Linda was exceptionally pretty, far too much so for her own good.'

'Any boyfriends you know about?'

Belling shook his head. 'I only ever saw her around with Tracey, but that doesn't mean much; I didn't know her that well.'

'What ever happened to Linda's mother? I'd always thought that multiple sclerosis wasn't a fatal condition.'

'You'll have to ask Charles Crichton about that – he's the Baines's GP and, incidentally, a quite excellent man.'

'How do you think Baines is going to take the death of his wife on top of Linda's murder?'

'George has always been a fighter and I don't think he's going to stop being one now. He's also had a long time to prepare himself for Rose's death. It wasn't unexpected – she was in very poor shape for several months before it happened.'

'We'll certainly need to see him soon; may I ring you tomorrow to find out how he is?'

'Of course.'

'Thank you very much and also for all your help.'

'Any time you want it, you only have to ask.'

The two detectives walked back along the drive, admiring the avenue of chestnuts.

'Quite some place,' Sinclair said, 'but I can't imagine how anyone can afford to keep it up these days. I don't know about you, but I rather took to our friend Belling.'

'So did I and it also sounds as if Linda Baines did as well.'

Sinclair nodded. 'And if she was playing havoc with the local males, it's my instinct that one of them was responsible for her death.'

'Or one of their wives, which might just possibly explain why a simulated rape was set up.'

'Or, indeed, one of their wives. Now, I think I'll take a stroll round the town to get the lie of the land and perhaps you'd make your number with the fellows at the local station and find out, if you can, the name of the woman who found Linda's body – I'd like a word with her before too long.'

As they entered the village Sinclair caught sight of the pub in the main street. He pulled into its car park.

'This looks like a convenient place to leave the car and I see that they do bar meals. Why don't we meet here at about one?'

'And what can I do for you, miss?'

The sergeant on the desk at Welbury police station was a powerfully built, but comfortable-looking, middle-aged man, who shook his head when Fiona had explained who she was and why she had come.

'Bad business that. Why don't you come through to the back room and have a cup of coffee while I get hold of Fred Grimes? He was the one who went to the scene of the murder.'

'That would be great, but are you sure it won't be taking him away from anything else?'

The man laughed. 'He's just nipped out in the patrol car to visit his missus in the cottage hospital. Her baby's due any time now and it's their first.' He raised his eyebrows. 'Anyone'd think that it had never happened to anyone else the way he's been carrying on.'

'But surely he won't want to leave her now.'

'Be good for 'em both. I reckon it's a false alarm – she'll be back home tomorrow, if you ask me.'

The station was hardly a hive of activity, Fiona thought, the sergeant coming back a few minutes later with a couple of mugs of coffee and being only too happy to chat.

'Did you know the poor girl who was killed?'

'Linda? Oh yes, I knew Linda all right – right tearaway she was, but she didn't deserve a fate like that, poor girl.'

'In what way was she a tearaway?'

'Up to all sorts of mischief; she scrumped apples when she was younger, she used to drink a bit, and a few weeks ago she did a streak at our May holiday cricket match. I was the one who had to hustle her away and you can imagine the teasing I had to put up with after that.'

'What did you do about it?'

'I know what I'd like to have done and that's to have warmed up that plump little rump of hers and may be that's what poor old George should have done long ago, but of course I couldn't and didn't. I gave her a talking to, but it did about as much good as my previous efforts in that direction and so I asked both Sir Geoffrey and Dr Crichton to have a word with her as well.'

'And did they?'

'Oh yes, and it seemed at least to have achieved something – she came round to apologize to me.'

'Did Mr Baines get to hear about it?'

'I don't think so, even though it caused quite some sensation in the village at the time. I managed to persuade Alan Seymour to keep it out of the *Welbury Chronicle* and although George used to enjoy a pint at the Green Man, in the last six months he's hardly left his house and unless someone took it upon themselves to go round and tell him, or else ring him up, the local paper would have been the only way for him to have found out.'

'Surely no one would have wanted to stir up trouble when he was having such a bad time at home.'

'I wouldn't be so sure. Every small town has its quota of

busybodies and do-gooders, but for once they seem to have decided to leave him in peace.'

'Was Sir Geoffrey at the cricket match?'

'Oh yes, he was there all right, but something like that wouldn't worry him: it was entirely thanks to him that the match got going again after it happened. He's very much the local squire is Sir Geoffrey, on all the committees, chairman of the bench and all that, but he's a good sort.' He looked up as he heard the car in the yard behind the station. 'That'll be Fred. I expect you'd like to see the place where it happened.'

'Yes, please, if you're quite sure it won't be too much trouble.'

'Trouble? It would be a pleasure.'

Fred Grimes didn't seem to be finding the imminent arrival of his first-born too much of a strain, Fiona thought, as she chatted to him in the Corsa.

'I'm sorry to have taken you away from the hospital.'

The ginger-haired young man turned towards her with a cheerful grin on his heavily freckled face.

'To be honest, it's a relief. Nothing's going on and I hate hospitals. You won't tell anyone, will you, but I wish it would all happen when I'm not there; these days everyone expects you to be on hand the whole time and I know that I'll faint or do something stupid when the moment arrives. At least Dr Crichton's on my side, but Dawn's been reading all those magazines and seems to think that the baby'll be scarred for life if I'm not with her when he arrives. I tell you one thing, if I'm the first thing the poor perisher sees, he really will be scarred for life.'

'It might be a girl.'

'No such luck. Dawn had to have one of those ultrasound things and we've known what make it's going to be for some time.'

'Do you like Dr Crichton?'

'Lovely man, which is more than I can say about his wife.'

'Why? What's wrong with her?'

'The booze.' He pointed through the window as they drove up the main street. 'That's their house.'

It was a most attractive house, with bow-windows and a tracery of ivy on its walls and was substantially built, with a walled courtyard to its side. Through the large double wooden gates, Fiona saw the Volvo estate car, then they were past it and climbing the slope out of the town.

'We came in this way from Sir Geoffrey's place.'

'Then you must have passed the spot where Linda was killed.'

'I didn't realize that.'

'Yes. it's about half-way between the village and the Hall.'

He drove on for another five minutes and then slowed to a standstill. They got out of the Corsa and Grimes pointed to the side of the road.

'It hasn't rained at all since it happened and you see that yellow mark on the grass?' Fiona nodded. 'The forensic blokes took a big stone away from there and I heard one of them saying that Linda must have hit her head on it when she was knocked off her bike.'

'And those are the tracks made when she was dragged away from the road?'

'That's right. Miss Pargeter found her through there.'

'Miss Pargeter?'

'Yes, she's one of the local characters, she lives in a cottage on the edge of the town – we passed it on our way out. There's no nonsense about Miss Pargeter; she stopped a passing car, told the driver to report to the station and then stood guard with her dog until I arrived. When I got there I radioed the station and waited until the chief super, the scene-of-crime men and the pathologist showed up.'

They walked through to the spot where the body had lain and Fiona looked at it, picturing the scene in her mind's eye. In a funny sort of a way, if Rawlings was right, it seemed almost worse that Linda hadn't been raped. At least, in that case, her death might have been the result of some uncontrollable impulse, but this looked so calculated, particularly as the pathologist seemed certain that she had been struck deliberately by the stone. She said as much to Sinclair after Grimes had taken her back to the Green Man.

'Yes,' I agree with you. Shall we go in?'

The middle-aged man behind the bar who, in his neat blue blazer and tan slacks, looked as if he was the proprietor, put down the glass he had been polishing as the two detectives came in.

'Good afternoon,' Sinclair said. 'I see that you do meals.'

'We do indeed. Baked potatoes with various fillings, chicken-and-leek pie with vegetables, pâté and ham or cheese ploughman's.'

'Hmm. I think I'll have the pie with French bread and butter and a glass of lager . How about you, Fiona?'

'The same with apple juice, please.'

The only other people in the saloon bar were a couple of men who were talking earnestly together at a table in the far corner by the window. When the landlord came back with their drinks after having given the lunch order to someone through the hatch in the wall behind the bar, Sinclair showed him his warrant card.

'We're looking into the murder of that girl, Linda Baines, last Sunday, and as a start we're trying to get a rough idea of life in the town. Have you been here long yourself?'

'No, Doris and I only took this place over three months ago.'

'How do you like it?'

'Very much so far; it's been very quiet up to now, but that suits us both well enough.'

'So you haven't got to know anyone much yet.'

'No, but from my short experience I reckon the people most likely to be able to help you are Sir Geoffrey Belling, Dr Crichton and Mr Atherton. The first two made a point of dropping in to see us when we first arrived, which was very civil of them.'

'I know about them, but who's Mr Atherton?'

'The local vicar. I gather that he's been here for the best part of twenty years. Not that I've met him – he doesn't approve of strong drink and on my side, you might say that religion is not one of my major interests.'

'What about Linda Baines? Did you know her at all?'

The man shook his head. 'Just who she was. She tried to get a drink in here soon after we arrived. One mustn't speak ill of the dead and all that, but she was a right bit of gaol-bait, at least on that occasion. She was all tarted up with make-up and long dangly earrings and looked all of nineteen.'

'Was she with anyone?'

'No, that's one of the reasons I remember her. She came in and stood at the entrance looking round, for all the world like one of the street girls who used to plague us at our previous pub in Nottingham, then she came up to the bar and asked for a gin and tonic.'

'Did you serve her?'

'No, fortunately not. Fred Grimes, one of the local police officers, who's a regular here, came out of the toilet at that moment and told her to push off.' The man looked round on hearing the sound from behind the hatch. 'That'll be your lunch. Would you like it at the bar or on one of the tables?'

'I think over there by the window.'

'Right you are, I'll bring it across for you.'

When he had finished eating Sinclair dabbed his lips with a paper napkin and gave an appreciative nod.

'That was really good, I must say. A pudding for you, Fiona?'

'No, thank you, just coffee, please.'

'I think I'll do the same.'

He took the plates up to the bar and came back with the cups of coffee a few minutes later. 'She certainly seems to have been a bit of a handful, does young Linda.'

'She certainly does.'

Sinclair nodded once or twice as Fiona told him what the sergeant had said about the girl's streak on the cricket field.

'I think it's about time we had a female view of her as well,' he said, when they were outside. 'Would you see what you can find out at the school and I'll take a wander round and have a chat to the woman who found Linda's body. Were you able to discover her name?'

'Yes, she's a Miss Pargeter and she lives in the last cottage on the left up that way.'

'Good work. Why don't we meet back here at about five?'

Sinclair watched as Fiona walked down the main street, then turned and began to stroll in the opposite direction.

He had intended to go straight to the cottage, but paused when he saw the church.

Although it looked to him as if at least part of it was Norman it was in a fine state of repair and the graveyard was in immaculate order, the grass being trimmed and fresh flowers placed on many of the graves.

Sinclair tried the door, not really expecting it to be unlocked, but it swung open as he gave it a push. He stepped inside. It took a moment or two before his eyes adapted to the gloom and then he looked round, his gaze being drawn to the organ loft.

'You'll no doubt be the detective from Oxford.'

Sinclair turned to see a tall, thin man wearing a black cassock, standing a few feet away. He had a very pale, lined face and his hair was cropped so short as to have left a mere dusting of grey over his scalp.

'News travels fast in these parts.'

The man didn't respond to the detective's smile, but did take his outstretched hand.

'And you must be Mr Atherton.'

'Yes, Cyril Atherton.'

'Mark Sinclair.'

Determined not to be ruffled by the man's unfriendly manner, the detective looked round again and pointed towards the altar.

'A very fine church you have here: the east end's Norman, isn't it, and the tower Perpendicular?'

The parson's expression softened a little. 'That is correct.'

'Although I've lived near Oxford for quite a few years now, I've not been to Welbury before and it's an omission I'm very glad to have been able to rectify.'

'I doubt very much, though, if you came here to study

architecture, or even to worship. You'd better come into the vestry if we're going to discuss Linda Baines – I imagine that's what you've come to see me about.'

The room was almost bare of furniture, with wooden cupboards around the walls, a table and some plain chairs set in the middle of the floor. In one corner there was a small basin with a water heater above it.

'Cigarette?'

'No, thank you.'

'You won't mind if I do?'

'Go ahead.'

'Tell me, Inspector,' Atherton said, when they were seated opposite each other, 'do you believe in evil?'

'I certainly think that there are wicked people, who are born and not made, but perhaps you didn't mean that.'

'Some people have the devil in them and Linda Baines was one of them. She was truly evil; she was an evil influence in her home, she was an evil influence on the young people here and she was an evil influence on the community as a whole.'

'I understand that she was only fifteen and that her mother had been disabled with a chronic and progressive illness for a good five years.'

'Are you meaning to imply that her age and problems at home are excuses for behaviour like hers?'

'If you would care to explain what sort of behaviour you are referring to, I might be able to comment.'

As soon as he had made the remark, Sinclair realized just how pompous it must have sounded, but Atherton didn't appear to have noticed anything.

'Any normal child with a disabled mother would have helped around the house, not spent her time hanging around the town corrupting the local boys.'

'Corrupting?'

'I detect a note of scepticism in your voice, Inspector, but then you never saw her in action – she even desecrated this church.'

'In what way?'

'I can hardly bring myself to tell you. She and one of the boys were pleasuring each other with their hands during my choir practice, in my church, in God's church. In Romans I, St Paul wrote: "wherefore God also gave them up to uncleanness through the lusts of their own hearts, to dishonour their own bodies between themselves." And in specific reference to women: "for even their women did change the natural use into that which is against nature."'

'But wasn't a lot of that referring to homosexuality?'

'And do you think we're immune to that in this village? Why, there's that "woman" Roberta Pargeter living in blatant immorality with another of the same sex not four hundred yards from here. And we're not spared drunkeness, either. There was an unseemly row between the doctor's wife and Miss Pargeter at the fête organized to raise money for the restoration of the organ, when they accused each other of the very vices I have mentioned. They did not hesitate to use the most intemperate language, either.'

'What did you do about Linda and the boy?'

'I threw them both out of the choir. The boy got a good hiding from his father, but not Linda, oh, dear me no. Baines refused to see me and even got Belling to try to intercede with me on her behalf. The final insult, not long after, was her disgusting display at the cricket match. I was umpiring and she deliberately flaunted herself in front of me in all her brazen nakedness. I have to admit that at that moment retribution was in my mind, but then I remembered St Paul's other words in his epistle to the

Romans. "Dearly beloved, avenge not yourselves, but rather give place unto Wrath; for it is written, Vengeance is mine; I will repay, saith the Lord."' Atherton gave the detective a piercing look. 'And so it came to pass.'

'Do I understand you to mean that you believe Linda's death to have been a form of divine retribution?'

Atherton licked his lips. '"God moves in a mysterious way ..."'

'But if I remember correctly,' Sinclair said, 'in the Olney hymns, Cowper also wrote:

"And every door is shut but one,
And that is mercy's door."

'The mercy in this case is that Linda Baines is no longer here to cause untold misery to the people of this parish; her fate is now in the hands of God.'

'And have you any idea who might have been the earthly instrument of retribution?'

'As far as I am concerned that chapter is closed and I have no intention of reopening it by indulging in idle speculation.'

'Did you visit Rose Baines when she was ill?'

'My presence in the Baines household was not welcome.'

'Why was that?'

'They were not believers.'

'So there won't be a funeral service, then?'

'Funeral services in my church are for those who believe in God.'

'If that view extends to the church's other activities, I am intrigued to know why Linda was in your choir.'

'She joined the youth club and I formed the opinion that

she was genuine in her desire to find the road to God through Christ. Sadly, I was wrong in my judgement.'

'Have you been here long?'

'Nearly twenty years.'

'And before that?'

'I was a missionary in Uganda.'

'Quite a difference.'

The man nodded sombrely. 'In many ways, my ministry here has been the more difficult task. Opposition and direct obstruction were challenges which I could understand and got used to tackling and overcoming, but apathy is altogether a more destructive element. Sin, too, committed in ignorance, is not so heinous as that undertaken in the full knowledge of its wickedness.'

'Leaving Uganda must have been a very difficult decision for you to take.'

'It was taken for me in the shape of tuberculosis. Had I not become ill, I would have stayed.'

'Why here, might I ask?'

'The bishop of this diocese was also a missionary in his younger days.'

'I see.'

Sinclair exerted all his very considerable personal charm to get Atherton talking about his time in Uganda and after a few minutes the man became quite animated, two spots of colour appearing on his pallid cheeks. He gradually began to unbend, showed the detective around the church and listened appreciatively when Sinclair tried out the organ.

'You must play for us one Sunday,' he said as they shook hands at the door. 'It's long been my ambition to get hold of a good organist.'

CHAPTER FOUR

Sinclair made his way slowly up the road from the church, pausing at the gate of the cottage, which was set back a few yards from the road. The front garden was a blaze of colour from the roses, which were in full bloom, as was the wisteria on the wall by the front door. The detective had just lifted the latch when he saw the figure kneeling behind the large rhododendron, which had been hiding her.

'Miss Pargeter?'

The thin, frail-looking woman, who was wearing a heavy jumper and thick skirt, despite the warmth of the day, peeled off her gardening-gloves and put her trowel into the trug beside her before slowly straightening up and facing the detective.

'No, she's out at the moment. Can I help you? I'm Amelia Pelton and I share the cottage with Roberta.'

'My name is Sinclair, Inspector Sinclair, and I just wanted a quick word with her as I understand that she was the one who found the body of the young girl who was murdered.'

'She shouldn't be too long. Would you like to come in for a cup of tea while you wait?'

'That would be most welcome.'

'Splendid. Do come in here – I won't be long.'

The living-room was comfortably untidy with an upright piano against one wall, a massive roll-top desk opposite and two leather armchairs on either side of the fireplace. On the mantelpiece there was a clock, a china ornament, a couple of invitations and a framed photograph. Sinclair was looking at the picture of a young woman wearing the uniform of a WRNS officer, when he heard a sound at the door and Miss Pelton came in wheeling a trolley.

'That was Roberta, taken during the war – she was on Mountbatten's staff in South East Asia Command. She looks very grand, doesn't she?'

'Most imposing. Have you lived here long?'

'Roberta was born in Welbury – her father was a very well-known local solicitor – and I joined her not long after the war. We met in India in fact. I was in the QAs and nursed her through a nasty attack of typhoid.'

'So you both must know a lot about Welbury.'

'Roberta's the one you should talk to. There's precious little that goes on around here without her knowing about it.'

'How about you?'

The woman gave a half-smile. 'I'm very happy looking after the garden and the flowers at the church. Roberta tells me all the news when she gets home. I can't think where she's got to; on golf days she's almost always back by this time.'

'So she's a golfer, is she?'

'Spoken like a fellow-sufferer, I reckon.'

Sinclair turned and got to his feet as a thickset woman advanced towards him with her hand outstretched.

'You must be the policeman.'

'That's right. Mark Sinclair.'

'I had a drink with Geoffrey Belling at the club and he told me you were here. Pelton looking after you properly?'

'Very well indeed, thank you.'

Sinclair resisted the considerable temptation to massage his fingers, which were aching from the effects of the woman's crunching handshake, and smiled.

'I gather that it was you who found Linda Baines's body.'

'That's right. I was taking Louis for a walk in the woods and we came across her just like that.'

'Louis?'

The woman gave a whistle and the honey-coloured Labrador ambled in, wagging its tail and going up to the detective, who rubbed the side of its neck.

'He's an old softy, not like his namesake Lord Louis. Comes with me on the golf-course and is as good as gold.'

'I'm very interested in Linda Baines and I was wondering if you might be able to tell me anything about her.'

'I haven't time now – got one of those bloody committee meetings at the hospital in half an hour and it wouldn't do to be late, I'm the chairperson. Bloody silly word, if you want my opinion, but one must keep up with the times – at least that's what Pelton's always telling me. Any chance of you coming to the golf-club tomorrow? I'm playing in the quarter-finals of the knock-out competition, and with a start time of eight-thirty we should be through by eleven; like me, my opponent likes to get on with it, thank God! I'll even stand you a coffee, or something stronger, if you like, and I'll also tell you anything you want to know about Linda and the other murky secrets of this sink of iniquity for good measure.'

'Roberta!'

'Be quiet, Pelton, or I might add you to my list as well.'

'All right,' Sinclair said, 'it's a deal.'

The woman looked at the trolley. 'Chocolate biscuits! You know I can't stand 'em. What are things coming to, Pelton? Fruit-cake is what I need and none of your genteel slices, either.'

'I'm sorry, Roberta, you were so late, I thought you would probably have had tea at the club.'

'Excuses, excuses. Look sharp, woman, can't you see that I'm suffering from near terminal hypoglycaemia?'

Sinclair finished his cup of tea and put it down on the trolley.

'That was excellent,' he said, 'but I really must be on my way. My assistant will be wondering what's happened to me.'

'You won't be late tomorrow, will you? Punctuality is one of my things.'

'I wouldn't dream of it.'

Sinclair found Fiona sitting in the lounge bar of the Green Man writing up some notes.

'How did you get on?' he asked.

'It was quite interesting, really.'

'Why not tell me about it? It won't do any harm to wait for half an hour or so to avoid the worst of the rush hour, unless, of course, you're in a hurry.'

'No, I've got nothing on this evening.'

'Miss Pembleton's the one most likely to be able to help you,' Alan Hartley, the headmaster of Welbury Comprehensive School, said after Fiona had introduced herself. 'She's in charge of PE and also takes an interest in counselling, so she probably saw more of Linda than anyone else here, particularly as Miss Renfrew, who was her class teacher last year, left us in the summer.'

'Did Linda need counselling, then?'

'Not specially, but when a child's mother is as disabled as Rose Baines was we like to try to forestall trouble. I'll get hold of her if you like and you can use that interview room over there.'

'Won't she be busy?'

'Yes, but this is more important than anything else at the moment and I know she won't mind. Linda's death has shaken us all very badly indeed. Although we take quite a lot of children from the surrounding villages, even so, it's a tight little community, this, with everyone more or less knowing everyone else.'

Christine Pembleton was a slim, athletic-looking woman in her late twenties, who was wearing a tracksuit and trainers.

'How can I help you?' she asked, when she had introduced herself.

'Well, I want to find out as much as I possibly can about Linda. We think it quite likely that her murderer was someone she knew, which means, if we're right, that it's vital for us to discover if there are any clues to what happened in her previous behaviour.'

'Yes, I see. Have you spoken to anyone else about her?'

'Only Sir Geoffrey Belling and the local police sergeant.'

'And what did they have to say?'

'Just that she was a bit of a handful at home.'

'Linda was all right – I was very fond of her, in fact. It's true that she did get up to all sorts of mischief, but a lot of the pranks were inspired by Tracey Farrell.'

'Sir Geoffrey mentioned her. Isn't she the daughter of his head gardener?'

'Yes, and a perfectly horrid child. She's about the same age as Linda was, but you'd never guess it to look at her – she'd pass for twelve. It's not only that; she's very plain with glasses and sticking-out ears and she used to get a buzz out of daring Linda to do all sorts of things. To give you an example, it was Tracey's idea to tie one of those blow-up sex dolls to the chimney in the old block, but it was Linda who did the climbing and took all the blame.'

'What about sex? Do you think that Linda was promiscuous?'

'What makes you ask that?'

'She seems to have been something of an exhibitionist from what I've heard.'

'You're talking about her streak, I suppose. Well, she certainly wasn't shy about her body, unlike most girls of that age. Dr Crichton carries out regular medical checks on all the children here and although I'm always present, some of them can hardly bear to have a stethoscope put under their vests. Linda wasn't like that, though; she'd strip off without any hesitation at all, but that's one thing and being promiscuous is quite another.

'I teach biology here as well as PE and I also handle sex instruction. As you can imagine with child abuse being so much in the news, I keep a special eye on the very badly behaved and very quiet ones and I did have a number of chats with Linda. In her case, though, it wasn't sex that I was worried about, but her home situation. Poor Mr Baines did his best, I'm sure, but during the last three years he hasn't been able to attend any of the parent/teacher meetings, although I must admit that he did take the trouble to come to see me specially on a couple of occasions. I think Linda badly missed his support at school activities, particularly athletics, at which she was exceptionally good. She held the school record for the high jump and had she had the motivation, I think she could have been really good.'

'Did you ever go round to the Baines's house?'

'Yes, I did once. Linda's class teacher wanted to talk to him about GCSEs and as I was the only member of staff to have met him she persuaded me that it would be easier if I made the initial approach. To be honest, she was just chickening out – Baines's temper is something of a byword in Welbury.'

'Did you also discuss Linda's behaviour with him?'

'That's what he came to see me about at the school and I intended to again – that's the real reason why I agreed to go to his house – but our conversation kept being interrupted by his having to go upstairs to attend to his wife and the poor man looked so tired and depressed that I didn't have the heart to bring it up.'

'Did Linda have a regular boyfriend?'

'Certainly not one of the lads at the school – one soon gets to hear about that. Quite honestly, I doubt whether she had one at all.'

'So you don't think she was having sex with anyone?'

'I don't see why, just because the poor girl was raped, it should be assumed that she was sexually free and easy. I don't think she was in the least, just high-spirited and lacking parental control, that's all.'

The atmosphere had suddenly become distinctly frosty and Fiona decided to change the subject.

'Is there a photograph of Linda here that I might take away with me?'

'I expect the school secretary would be able to help you.'

'And one last thing.'

'Yes?'

The tone of voice remained icy, but Fiona did her best to ignore it.

'Do you think I might have a word with Tracey Farrell?'

'I'll ask the secretary to get hold of her.'

Fiona had to admit that Christine Pembleton was quite

right about Tracey; the girl was indeed extremely plain and made absolutely no attempt to improve on nature. Her hair, which was badly in need of a good wash, was scraped back into a pony-tail, which accentuated her prominent ears and also revealed the whole expanse of her forehead, which was studded with adolescent spots.

'Hello,' Fiona said, giving the girl a smile. 'I'm Fiona Campbell, thank you for coming. Why not sit down over there?'

The girl stared at her for a moment, then did so, perching right on the edge of the chair.

'I expect you know that I'm a police officer and that I'm looking into Linda's death. You were her special friend, weren't you?' The girl nodded. 'I understand that Linda told her father that she was going to meet you on the afternoon she was killed.'

'I didn't see her at all – I went for a long ride on my bike.'

Perhaps it was because of the way she answered so quickly, or because, having been staring at her through her metal-framed glasses, the girl suddenly dropped her eyes, that Fiona was convinced that she was lying and decided to back her hunch.

'Do you know what obstructing the police in the course of their enquiries means?'

The girl didn't look up and began to fiddle with the hem of her skirt.

'I'm sure you do, but what you probably don't know is that people can be put in prison for doing it, in your case, youth custody, and you wouldn't like that, would you? You did meet Linda that afternoon, didn't you, and she had sex with someone, didn't she?'

Fiona hadn't been absolutely certain about it before, but

she was now; the girl in front of her had gone ashen pale and a tear began to run slowly down her cheek.

'Tell me exactly what happened and I promise you that you won't get into any trouble.'

'You won't say anything to my dad, will you? You don't know him – he'd kill me if he found out about it.'

'No, I won't, provided you tell me the truth.'

Tracey Farrell hesitated for a moment, brushed the tear away and then nodded.

'Have you ever done it, Linda?'

'What are you on about now?'

'You know, had it off with a bloke.'

'That would be telling, wouldn't it?'

'I don't believe you have – you wouldn't dare.'

Tracey Farrell licked her lips, already feeling the excitement beginning to build up, as it always did when she saw Linda making the familiar gesture that meant she had taken the bait. Her friend tilted her head back and stared straight at her.

'There's nothing to it – I've done it loads of times.'

'It's easy enough to say that. I still don't believe you.'

'What do you bet?'

'If you can prove it, you can have my silver bracelet. You know, the one you like so much with all the ornaments on it.'

'All right, you're on. What proof do you want?'

Tracey held her breath for a moment and then let it out very slowly.

'I'd have to see you do it.'

'What?'

'That's the only proof I'll accept.'

'That's ridiculous.'

'Chicken! I knew it was all talk.'

'Nobody calls me chicken.'

'You'll do it, then?'

'I'll think about it.'

Tracey knew she had won and that it was now only a question of time. The streak had been exciting enough, but this would put that into the shade. Having got Linda's agreement, it would now be a question of encouragement, of telling her how terrific she was and brave and of working out the details.

After a great deal of thought Tracey introduced the name of a possible partner a few days later.

'You know how you've often told me how much you fancied Phil – how about him? You've seen the way he looks at you and you told me how disappointed you were that he didn't partner you in the obstacle race.'

'We'd have to be careful – I don't fancy being caught by Mr Rouse.'

Tracey didn't, either. Rouse was Sir Geoffrey's farm manager, a surly man with a notorious temper, quite unlike his son Phil, who was working as a gardener while waiting to go to agricultural college. He always had a cheery word for them and was a good-looking young man, with curly fair hair and an engaging grin.

'I'll find out when Mr Rouse is next away and then we could use the summer-house – no one ever goes near there on a Sunday.'

The more Tracey thought about it, the better the idea seemed to be. Sir Geoffrey had let them use the summer-house for some time as a den; it was in a secluded part of the grounds, it was dry, there were cushions and rugs in it and they even had a key, which they kept hanging on a hook under the eaves. Even better, there was a loose knot of wood in the back wall, which could easily be prised out and she would be able to watch the proceedings without any fear of detection.

Their chance came when Tracey discovered that Rouse and Sir Geoffrey were going to an exhibition of agricultural machinery in Birmingham the following weekend and were not expected back until late on the Sunday afternoon. Half the challenge now was to get Phil there without either frightening him or arousing his suspicions and she was still wondering how to set about it when she found out that that Sunday was also Phil's birthday. Was that piece of luck a good omen? She fervently hoped so. Tracey was hardly able to eat any lunch that day and was feeling sick with nervous anticipation as she waited behind the summer-house. Through the hole in the wall she could see Linda sitting on one of the cushions and then at the same moment as she heard the loud creak from the door, her friend started to get to her feet.

There was no feeling of envy as she watched Linda peeling off her jumper and shirt and then pulling down her jeans. It was as if she was the slim girl with the trim waist and shiny black hair, who was facing the young man. She saw his eyes widen as Linda reached up behind her to unhook her bra and then slowly began to ease her pants down over her hips.

'Come on, Phil, it's your turn now.'

Tracey knew all about the mechanics of sex, but nothing she had read or heard about had prepared her for what she could see in front of her. Phil was enormous, terrifyingly so. Surely, she thought, he would be bound to do Linda a serious injury. Forty-five minutes later, when Phil left, Tracey was utterly exhausted. Her muscles ached from having been on tiptoe for so long and the images she had seen and the sounds she had heard were still sending shivers of nervous excitement right through her.

Tracey waited until Linda had finished dressing. When she went into the summer-house her friend was running a comb through her hair.

'Satisfied?' All Tracey could do was nod. 'How about that bracelet then?'

'I'll let you have it tomorrow. Are you all right?'

'Of course I'm all right. What are you on about now?'

'But wasn't it terribly painful?'

'Painful? Of course it wasn't. It was great, really good, the best ever.'

'It sounded as if you were being torn apart.'

'Don't be stupid. It adds to it if you can make a bit of noise.'

'I didn't know that a bloke could do it twice straight off like that.'

Linda giggled. 'Neither did I. Perhaps it's only possible for someone young.'

'But weren't you taking a frightful risk?'

'What do you mean?'

'Well, he wasn't wearing one of those things, was he?'

'What do you take me for, Tracey? I'm not looking to get in the family way, if that's what you're worrying about. How do I look?'

'Fine.'

She looked a great deal better than fine, Tracey thought; her friend's cheeks were glowing and her eyes were sparkling as she turned away.

'Where are you going?'

'Wouldn't you like to know?'

'What time did she leave you?' Fiona asked.

'I didn't look at my watch, but it must have been about four-thirty.'

'And that was the last you saw of her?'

'Yes. She picked up her bike which she had left in the trees behind the summer-house and went off down the track and out by the back way.'

'Where does that lead to?'

'There's a lane which goes past the farm and joins the main road.'

'Would you draw a sketch for me?'

The girl did so on a blank page in Fiona's notebook and when she had finished, pushed her chair back.

'May I go now?'

'Yes, but I may need to see you again.'

'You really won't tell my father, will you?'

'No, I won't, but only if you promise me that you won't mention the details of our conversation to anyone and by anyone, I mean anyone and, what's more, stick to that promise. No one at school here, not a friend, not Phil Rouse, not anyone in your family.' The girl nodded. 'I want to hear you say it.'

'I promise.'

Fiona closed her notebook and looked at Sinclair across the table.

'You did an excellent job with that girl,' he said, 'she sounds an absolute horror.'

'Yes, but what she said had the ring of truth about it.'

'And it also explains Rawlings's findings.'

'What I can't understand is why Linda didn't go home straight after that summer-house business. The shortest way would have been through Sir Geoffrey's garden and even if she went out the back way to avoid being seen, she would have had to go in the opposite direction from that leading to the lodge and through the town to have reached the spot where she was found. Look, you can see on Tracey's sketch.'

'Yes, that does seem odd.'

'I'm afraid I didn't exactly shine with that PE teacher, though. I thought that if I were to tell her about Rawlings's view that Linda hadn't been raped and was sexually experienced, it would be all round the town tomorrow and yet, without doing so, it obviously looked as if I was trying to make out that she was raped because she was promiscuous and that didn't go down at all well.'

'Don't worry, I think you were quite right to keep quiet about it. Now about tomorrow, I'm going to see the redoubtable Miss Pargeter, who, I suspect, knows pretty well everything that goes on around here and I was wondering if you would have a chat with Dr Crichton. The other thing we must do is to take a look at Linda's room. If you hang on here for a moment, I'll give Belling a ring and find out how Baines is.'

The detective came back several minutes later and sat down beside her again.

'That's all pretty satisfactory. Belling's got a spare key to the lodge and he's prepared to take the responsibility of letting us in tomorrow morning as evidently Baines is still in no sort of shape to discuss anything. I've arranged to pick it up at eight-thirty, which should give us plenty of time before my meeting with Miss Pargeter.'

CHAPTER FIVE

Sir Geoffrey Belling was waiting for them by the lodge as they drove in through the gates promptly at 8.30 the following morning and walked across to the car, making a gesture for Sinclair to lower the window.

'Good morning. Don't bother to get out,' he said, holding out a ring with two keys on it, a Yale and that of a mortice lock. 'George hasn't got up yet and I didn't feel it would be fair either to bother him with this last night, or wake him this morning; that's why I came to meet you down here.'

'Would you like to come into the lodge with us?'

'I'm quite sure that you wouldn't want me getting in your way.'

'All right, then, thank you. We shouldn't be very long and when we've finished I'll bring up the key to you at the Hall.'

The front door of the lodge opened straight into a good-sized living-room with a staircase on its left. To the right of the stone fireplace was a door leading into the kitchen. Everything was clean and tidy, the cushions on the sofa and easy-chairs were puffed up, Linda's homework on the table by the window was in a neat pile and the kitchen was spotless. The same was true of the double bedroom and

PETER CONWAY

the bathroom upstairs. The large bed had been stripped and covered with a candlewick bedspread, the camp-bed by its side had been folded up, the window was open a crack and there was an air-freshener on the sill. There was a third door leading off the landing and it failed to open when Sinclair tried it.

'That's curious,' he said. 'The place has obviously had a good clean recently. Why should Linda's bedroom be locked?'

'Adolescent girls sometimes do lock their bedroom doors; I don't suppose there was a key in the clothes she was wearing when she was killed.'

'No, there was nothing but a handkerchief in the pocket of her jeans. Well, I suppose I'd better give Belling a ring. While I do so perhaps you'd take a look at the bathroom.'

It didn't take Fiona long. There were a couple of towels on the rail, a flannel on the side of the bath, a shower-cap hanging on the hook behind the door, two toothbrushes and paste in a plastic beaker on the rim of the basin and a selection of creams, jars of make-up and a packet of paracetamol tablets in the glass-fronted cabinet above it. There was no sign of the medication, which surely, she thought, Mrs Baines must have been taking. Before leaving she opened the airing cupboard, which filled in the angle between the bath and the door, and looked inside.

Fiona was waiting for Sinclair on the landing when he came back up the stairs.

'Sorry I was so long. There were complications.'

'Oh?'

'Belling knew nothing about the door being locked and he's changed his mind about letting us look through Linda's room without Baines knowing. Evidently the man got up soon after we left and he's a lot better; he's also prone to flying off the handle and Belling thinks there might be an explosion from him if he knew we were down here. He suggests that we go back up to the Hall and talk to the man, without letting on that we've been here at all. He says he knows the fellow backwards and that he's sure he won't kick up a fuss if he's handled properly. He thinks he'll let us have the key without any difficulty if asked nicely. Incidentally, he doesn't want us up there for about ten minutes; he's proposing to tell Baines that we were ringing from the village.'

'It doesn't look as if we've got much choice but to agree,' Fiona said, 'unless we batter the door down, although, of course, I could always try a little magic.'

Before Sinclair could reply, she walked up to the door and knocked three times.

'Open, Sesame! Hmm, even that doesn't seem to have done the trick.'

She turned the handle, pushed and when the door swung open, stepped back. Her hand went to her mouth.

'Good God!'

Sinclair looked at her for a moment and then shook his head slowly.

'I'm not sure what the penalty is for taking the micky out of your elders, if not your betters – I'll have to think about it. Where did you find the key?'

Fiona grinned at him. 'In the airing cupboard in the bathroom. It was on a hook behind the jamb of the door between the top two shelves. If I hadn't climbed on to the chair in there and felt around, I'd have missed it.'

'Well done. This is too good an opportunity to miss, but in the interests of tact, we'll have to get the timing right.' He set the count-down on his watch. 'Let's have a general look around first.'

To a casual inspection, the room looked like that

belonging to any normal teenager; there were posters on the wall, a large mobile was hanging from the ceiling and a battered teddy bear was lying on the bedspread, which had been half-pulled up over the continental quilt; the wardrobe door was hanging open, a pair of pyjamas and some dirty underwear were on the floor and there was a jumble of cassettes and compact discs on the easy-chair.

'Right,' said Sinclair, 'would you have a look through her clothes and I'll tackle the bookcase and that chest.'

While Fiona made a start on the wardrobe Sinclair took each volume out one by one and flicked through the pages. When he had finished he was just beginning on the chest when the alarm on his watch went off. He looked across at Fiona who was just lifting up a pile of jumpers in the chest of drawers. He closed the heavy lid.

'I think we ought to go now.'

'Shall I shut the window?'

'No, I think that would be a mistake. Either Baines or Belling might have noticed it was open and I don't want them getting paranoid about us sneaking in here without permission.'

He locked the door, pocketed the key and then followed her down the stairs.

'Find anything unusual?' he asked as he started the car.

'Well, I didn't have anything like as long as I would have liked, but there were three things that stuck out like a sore thumb. What was a girl like Linda, whose father, if not exactly poor, is clearly not well off, doing with a designer-labelled sheepskin jacket, which must have cost a good five hundred pounds, and leather boots worth about a hundred? And that's not to mention the suede handbag and the hi-fi set.'

'What was the label on the jacket?'

'It just said "Rochelle – Oxford and London".'

'That mean anything to you?'

'I'm afraid not. Did you come up with anything?'

'Just three packets of contraceptive pills, one half-used, inside an old children's encyclopaedia, which had had its pages hollowed out to make room for them, and, as you said, the hi-fi equipment. I'm no great expert, but a midi-set like that with AM and FM radio, turntable, twin tape-deck, compact-disc player and top-class earphones, must have set her back a good five hundred pounds. I think it would be a good idea to get a scene-of-crime man to take a proper look this afternoon; he'd do a better job in thirty minutes than we would in a couple of hours.'

'Where do you suppose all that stuff came from?'

'I'd prefer to leave the speculation until there's been a proper search.'

Belling came up to the car as they pulled up outside the house and opened Fiona's door for her.

'I'm sorry, it must have been something of a wild-goose chase for you. What exactly were you looking for?'

'Nothing special,' Sinclair said, 'but more often than not rapists and murderers are known to their victims and it's possible that Linda kept a diary, or even some letters, which might give us a clue.'

'May I give you a friendly word of warning?' Sinclair smiled and inclined his head. 'George wouldn't take kindly to the suggestion that Linda might not have been as sexually innocent as he fondly imagined. Preoccupied as he was with Rose, I'm pretty certain he was insulated from most if not all of the gossip.'

'Thanks for the tip. Do you think, then, that she might have been up to more than just adolescent pranks?'

'I wouldn't be surprised.'

They found George Baines standing staring out of the window when they were shown into the study. Although the man was only of medium height, Sinclair noted his broad shoulders and massive forearms and he could also see that he was as tense as a tightly coiled spring.

'I realize just what a terrible time this is for you,' the detective said when the introductions had been made, 'but if we are to make any progress we need to pick up every possible clue, which is why we would like your permission to take a look at Linda's room.'

'That don't seem much of a reason to me.'

'It's just possible that she might have been going out to meet someone that afternoon and if so, she might have received a note.'

'Are you implyin' that Linda—'

'I'm not implying anything. As I said, we're just hunting for clues at the moment. You do want us to catch the person responsible for Linda's death, don't you?'

"Course I do; I just don't want you pryin' into 'er things, that's all. Anyway, you won't be able to get in; she kept 'er room locked an' I don't know where the key is.'

'Why did she do that?'

Baines looked round at his employer, who gave him an encouraging nod and made an almost imperceptible calming gesture with his hand.

'Abaht a year ago she told me that she'd like a corner of the house that was 'er own and not 'ave Mrs Webster pokin' into 'er things. I understood and respected 'er wish and in return, she promised to keep it clean.'

'Mrs Webster?'

'She's one of Sir Geoffrey's cleaning women and once Rose got bad she used to come to the lodge once a week to help me aht and collect the laundry.'

'It would help me a lot to get a picture of Linda from you, Mr Baines. What sort of girl was she?'

'Full of life and the outdoor type. She fahnd school work a bit of a problem, as I did at 'er age, but she was very good at athletics and also liked cyclin' and ridin'.'

'Did you find her difficult to deal with in any way?'

''Ow do you mean?'

'Coming in late, problems with drinking or boys, anything like that.'

'Linda could be rude at times and wasn't very helpful once 'er mother was confined to bed, but that's under-standable enough; I didn't 'ave as much time for 'er as I should 'ave and she must 'ave felt neglected. She weren't interested in boys, thank God, and didn't drink at all. 'Er only real friend was Tracey Farrell.'

'Some adolescent girls, even in this day and age, can be surprisingly ignorant about sex, which may get them into difficult situations quite unwittingly – had Linda had any sex instruction?'

Fiona had to admire Sinclair's technique. A few minutes earlier, Baines had been full of aggression and looking as if he would refuse to co-operate and now here he was answering sensitive questions without a hint of protest.

'Rose 'andled that side of things a long time ago, it was also done at school and magazines for teenagers these days don't leave much aht.'

'Did you give Linda much pocket-money?'

'No. For one thing I didn't think it was a good idea and for another, I couldn't afford to. She got five quid a week from me and made a bit extra with things like exercising Sir Geoffrey's 'orses, 'elping Miss Pelton with 'er garden and she also used to do a paper-rahnd when she was younger.'

'What did she do for clothes?'

'Linda didn't 'ave much time for 'em. She was always a bit of a tomboy and was usually in jeans and a T-shirt except when she 'ad to wear school uniform. I gave 'er a few things like 'er tracksuit and running-kit as presents and she'd tell me if she needed new underclothes and things like that.'

'Well, thank you for all your help, Mr Baines. I take it, then, that you'll have no objection if one of my men comes to look at Linda's room. I promise you he won't damage the door and we'll let you know if we find anything of importance.'

'I don't know, I ...'

'If you're worried about any personal matters or belongings, I can assure you that they will be treated with the strictest confidence and I have no objection to you or Sir Geoffrey being present when our man comes, if that would reassure you.'

'That's a good idea, George. If you'd like some support, you have only to say the word.'

'You couldn't 'andle it on your own, could you, sir? I think I would find it too upsettin'.'

'Of course. Only too pleased.'

'Fine,' said Sinclair. 'I'll ring our man now, if I may, and perhaps you'd bring the key to Linda's room with you, Sir Geoffrey, when he arrives. Would you mind if I use your phone?'

'Carry on. We'll leave you in peace here. Come along, George.'

Sinclair managed to locate one of the scene-of-crime men and told him to contact Sir Geoffrey before going to the lodge and to expect him to be present when he inspected the bedroom.

'I'll drop you off at Crichton's surgery if you like,' the detective said to Fiona as they approached the village a few minutes later.

'Don't bother, thanks, I can easily walk from here and it will save you time.'

'Don't worry about that and anyway, I must give Dobson another ring.'

'Oh, why?'

'To warn him not to let on to Sir Geoffrey if he finds anything and to arrange for him to meet me later on for his report. You're also no doubt wondering why I didn't tell him before and why I suggested that one or both of them should be present during the search.'

'Yes, I am.'

'I had an instinct that otherwise Baines would have created a fuss and I'm also a shade uneasy about Belling.'

'In what way?'

'Just that I'm pretty sure that whoever cleaned up the lodge would have told him that Linda's room was locked and if that was the case, why didn't he tell us straight away? In addition to that, someone picked up the extension while I was talking to Dobson, hence the need for another call. Right then, I hope that all goes well with Crichton. When you've seen him and typed up your notes, why not take the rest of today off, we may well have work at the weekend.'

The entrance to Dr Crichton's surgery was inside the courtyard of the GP's house and, the Volvo not being there, Fiona assumed that the morning surgery was over.

'I'm making enquiries into Linda Baines's death,' she said to the receptionist, who was sitting behind the counter on the right side of the lobby, after she had introduced herself, 'and as I gather that she was one of Dr Crichton's patients, I was wondering if I might have a word with him about her.'

'I'm sure he'd be only too pleased to do so,' the woman replied with a friendly smile. 'He went up to the hospital about half an hour ago, but I'm expecting him back any time now. Would you care to wait?'

'Yes, thank you.'

Fiona went through into the waiting-room and was still writing up her notes on their visit to the lodge and Hall, when a large, untidy-looking man in his late fifties with a rugged face and whose ears and nose suggested that he had either been a boxer or a Rugby player, came into the room. He had on a shapeless tweed suit with bulging pockets, but despite his superficially menacing appearance, his warm smile as he advanced across the room with his hand outstretched and his deep, melodious voice when he spoke, reassured her completely.

'Miss Campbell? I'm Charles Crichton. Look, I'd like nothing better than to see you now, but I'm going to a post-graduate meeting in Reading over lunch and there won't be time. Would you be free to meet me here for tea?'

'Thank you, I'd enjoy that.'

'Excellent. Come along at about four and just ring the front door bell of the main part of the house; my house-keeper, Hilda, will be expecting you. The afternoon surgery is a little unpredictable, but I should be through by then.'

After walking to the local station, Fiona did as Sinclair had suggested and, deciding that a break from Welbury would do her no harm at all took the bus back to Oxford, picked up her car and drove the few miles to Henley and, after lunch at a pub, took a brisk walk along the towpath, enjoying the sights and sounds of the river and putting thoughts of murder, rape, disturbed adolescents and distraught parents firmly out of her mind. Promptly at four, Fiona was back at Crichton's house and was shown into the drawing-room by an elderly, white-haired woman with a deeply wrinkled face and a stoop, who walked with a pronounced limp.

'What a lovely room this is!' Fiona said.

'Yes, it's the doctor's favourite and mine, too.'

'Have you been here a long time?'

'Bless you, yes. I was with Dr Crichton senior before Dr Charles was born. I don't expect he'll be long. Please make yourself comfortable. Are you sure you'll be all right? There are some magazines over there.'

'Thank you. Don't worry about me, you've already been most kind and I'm sure you've got plenty to do.'

'A pleasure, I'm sure.'

After the woman had left Fiona picked up a copy of *Country Life* and began to read an article on one of the new acquisitions of the National Trust.

'What the hell do you think you're doing here? This part of the house is private – the patients' waiting-room is through that door there.'

Fiona got to her feet to face the red-haired, angry-looking woman who was standing at the door. At first glance she seemed quite elegant, but when she approached Fiona could see that her stockings were wrinkled, her make-up clumsily applied and her nails bitten to the quick.

'Mrs Crichton, is it? I'm a police officer, I'm enquiring into Linda Baines's murder and your husband has invited me to have tea with him here. Didn't he tell you?'

The woman gave a mirthless laugh. 'My husband

wasn't expecting me back until later. A police officer? At least that's one I haven't heard before.'

Before Mrs Crichton had time to say anything further Fiona took her warrant card out of her handbag and held it out.

'God! You really are one, then?'

'Yes, I am.'

'Since when did they take to appointing gaol-bait to our revered police force? You needn't look at me like that and don't think you can nick me for drunken driving – I came back home in a taxi. Do you want me to give you the name of the firm?'

'You have a lovely house,' Fiona said, trying desperately to change the subject. 'I was just telling your housekeeper what a magnificent room this was.'

The woman peered at her, a puzzled expression on her face. 'So you've met hopalong Hilda, have you?' She took a few faltering steps towards the sofa and then sat down heavily on it. 'Do you know what it's like living in this god-forsaken dump?'

'I've never stayed in the country for any length of time, but I imagine it must get pretty claustrophobic at times.'

'Claustrophobic? It's a living death.' The woman began to fiddle with her rings, her fingers trembling. 'Oh yes, the future looked so exciting and to hold such promise when Charles was doing orthopaedic surgery at St Mary's, where I was a physiotherapist. He had played Rugby for Oxford and a few times for England, he was a senior registrar and looked set for a career as a London consultant. And then what did he do after we were married? He came to this dead-and-alive hole and took over his father's practice. Why did he do it? Don't ask me. He knew I desperately wanted to stay in London, but he had made up his mind and that was that – he can be very stubborn, can Charles. There was a good deal of talk about a country practice being his true vocation and a lot of twaddle like that, but I think he did it to spite me – he always resented my having a good time in London. Why didn't I refuse to come? Well, I'm talking about twenty-five years ago and my father made it clear that he wouldn't support me if I left Charles and I didn't fancy trying to make ends meet on a physiotherapist's pay. In his own way, my father's just as bad as my dear husband and he still exerts his influence. He lent Charles a great deal of money to build the surgery on to this house and buy the dirty great yacht that he races whenever he has the time, and my father, being Calvinistically inclined, doesn't approve of divorce or separation and would want the money back if anything unfortunate like that were to occur. Does Charles ever take me on the boat? Like hell, he does – "a mere woman like you would get in the way and would feel sick and scared whenever it got really rough, wouldn't you, dear?"

'And why am I telling you, a complete stranger, all this? It's because I'm drunk, if you hadn't realized it already. I've always been ever so discreet about it – I always buy the stuff in Reading so that I don't rock Charles's boat here in Welbury – but I don't know why I bother, you can't keep anything quiet in a small country town. It's all go here, you know. Do you know what Charles's idea of a rave-up used to be? It was to have the Bellings round for dinner. "Landed gentry, salt of the earth, finest chap I've ever met, don't yer know?" God, it used to make me sick. At least it stopped after Margot pegged out – she drank herself to death, as a matter of fact, and I don't blame her, I'm well on the way to doing the same thing myself.'

'Did you know Linda Baines?'

'Linda Baines! To hear my precious husband talk, you'd think she was St Theresa of Lisieux, but, believe me, she was nothing less than a slag. I could tell you things about her that would—'

'Helen!'

Charles Crichton's voice cut across the room like the crack of a whip and his wife's head jerked round.

'Helen, would you be good enough to ask Hilda to bring in the tea?'

Fiona hadn't heard him come in. How long had he been standing there, she wondered, and how much had he heard? She saw Helen Crichton's expression change from one of surprise to one of truculence, then her husband stepped in front of her, blocking her from view. It was all done skilfully and quickly and in other circumstances Fiona might have believed that he was helping her to the door, but in fact, he practically carried her across the room and outside, returning a minute or two later as if nothing had happened.

'Did you have a pleasant afternoon?'

'Yes, thank you. I went for a walk along the river at Henley.'

'Very wise. Why stay indoors on a beautiful day like this if you don't have to?'

Fiona had a feeling of complete unreality as they exchanged banalities until the housekeeper came in with the tea-trolley.

'Thank you, Hilda. My goodness, those scones look delicious and is that some of your raspberry jam?'

'Just as you like it, Dr Charles.'

'I don't know what I'd do without you, Hilda, I really don't.'

He gave the woman a warm smile, she then limped out of the room, shutting the door behind her.

'Hilda was my nanny and then my father's house-keeper. She must be all of eighty and is riddled with arthritis, but she hasn't lost her touch with the scones. Why not try one?'

'Thank you, I will.'

Charles Crichton took one himself, cut it in half, buttered it and then added a large blob of jam. When he had finished eating it, he put his plate down on the occasional table and looked across at her.

'Now, what is it you wanted to ask me about Linda?'

'I gather that she was often up to mischief and Sergeant Stringer told me that you'd had a chat with her after her streak.'

Crichton nodded. 'Not only then, but on a number of other occasions as well. I wouldn't want to give the wrong impression; there was nothing wrong with Linda that getting a year or so older wouldn't have cured. Her problems were mostly due to her mother's illness and George Baines's reaction to it. I'm not criticizng George, who was incredibly loyal and devoted to Rose, but you can't be a full-time nursemaid to your wife and also a single parent to a spirited adolescent.'

'I'd no idea that multiple sclerosis was such a lethal condition.'

'It usually isn't. Of course a GP like me only sees two or three cases during a career, but I was asking one of the neurologists at Oxford about it only the other day. In Rose's case, it had attacked her brainstem and affected her temperature control and the respiratory centre. It was the failure of that last that killed her – she just stopped breathing.'

'The forensic pathologist seems convinced that Linda was sexually experienced – there was no bruising of the vulva and no recent tears of the hymen.'

'With respect, I think that that is a lot of nonsense. I knew Linda and he didn't. In any case, most girls use tampons these days and she also did a lot of riding and athletics, so I don't see how he could be so sure. I gather, too, that she suffered a severe head injury and the rape may have occurred when she was unconscious, which might explain any absence of trauma to the genital region. No, I am aware that a lot of people here would say that Linda was sex obsessed and cite her streak as an example, but that was just done as a dare and was nothing more than a bit of mischief – she told me so herself. Later on she was really sorry that she had done it and after Geoffrey Belling had a word with her, she had the courage to apologize to Stringer.'

'Some adolescents must be very difficult to deal with.'

'They are. I'm the medical officer at the local school and have seen it all.'

'What do you do if an under-age girl comes to you and asks for the pill?'

'I don't need to tell you that for them to have sex is against the law and I almost always tell the parents. I know all about the debate with regard to confidentiality, but I think that a girl's health and future are more important than that. All I can say is that I've almost never regretted it. These days parents aren't involved nearly enough in the bringing up of adolescents and they need every encouragement to build up confidence in their ability to instil discipline and self-control.'

'Which is what Linda lacked?'

'Precisely.'

'Do you think that she was murdered by a local person?'

'Most unlikely in my view. I know the people here like the back of my hand – after all, I was born here – and I'd

82

stake my reputation on saying that there aren't any rapists or murderers here. No, I think it was an opportunistic crime. Someone driving through must have seen her cycling along and decided to act; rapists have cruised around and done just that often enough in the past.'

'So you know about the car?'

'Yes, Fred Grimes told me about it. I delivered his first child at the hospital early this morning as it happens.'

'All went well, I hope.'

'Yes. A fine seven-and-a-half-pound boy.'

'How do you think George Baines is going to cope with all this?'

'Too early to say. I was with him very soon after Rose died, which I think was some comfort, and he will have the support of Geoffrey Belling, but the thing that worries me most is his guilt over Linda.'

'Guilt?'

'Yes. He was already saying to me that if only he had had more time for Linda, she would have been less rebellious and would not have gone out on her bicycle that afternoon. Thoughts of the "if only" variety are very common in the recently bereaved, but problems can arise if they persist. Guilt is never, in my view, at all a happy emotion, particularly when it's not justified, and George is going to need all the support I can give him over the next few weeks.'

'Hasn't he got any family?'

'No one close, as far as I know, and Rose was an orphan.'

'Poor man. Well, thank you for all your help and for the delicious tea.'

'If I can do anything more, you know where to find me.'

The GP showed her to the front door and shook her by the hand.

'May I be so bold as to give you a word of advice?' he said as she was turning away. 'I've lived and worked in this town for a long time, and as in any small community there are a lot of people who enjoy a gossip. Linda, with some of her more high-spirited antics, made quite a few enemies and there will be those who will undoubtedly enjoy sticking the knife in. It might be wise to remember that when you are talking to people.'

Fiona had just put her key in the lock of her car which she had parked out of the way of Crichton's Volvo, when she heard footsteps on the gravel behind her and whirled round.

'Bit jumpy, aren't you?'

'Oh, it's you, Mrs Crichton.'

'Don't look so pleased to see me, will you? Aren't you going to open the door for me? I'm not going to stand here all bloody afternoon, you know.'

'I'm sorry.'

Once inside the car, the woman pulled up the sleeve of her jumper and showed Fiona the bruises on her forearm.

'My sweet, gentle husband was responsible for that. And do you know why? It was because I was just about to tell you a few home truths about the slutty Linda. You don't believe me, do you? Well, if it isn't true, why did he get into such a panic and pull me out of the room like that? It was because he didn't want you to know that she was always in the surgery for one reason or another and that he liked to give her bum a feel when he thought no one was looking. Ever so fatherly of him, wasn't it, to put an arm around her shoulders when he was showing her out? And what do you suppose went on in that consulting-room of his? Not just a quick feel, I can tell you. Any sensible GP takes a chaperon with him when he disappears into the examination room with a nymphet like her and, of course, Charles is normally most punctilious about that sort of thing, except, that is, when it was with dear Linda. You still don't believe me, do you? I didn't think you would, but it's all true.'

Fiona sat motionless in her car long after Helen Crichton had disappeared from view. Surely what the woman had been saying couldn't possibly be true, and yet someone had clearly been giving Linda expensive presents, or, she thought, been blackmailed into so doing.

CHAPTER SIX

Sinclair arrived at Welbury Park Golf Club a few minutes before eleven. When he went into the clubhouse he saw on the notice board that Roberta Pargeter and her opponent had the earliest start time of the eight couples playing. When the steward told him that the two women had not yet finished their match he strolled down the side of the eighteenth fairway and, as there was no one in sight, followed it back to the tee. The hole was a 368-yard par four for the ladies, and as it led uphill to a plateau green he could see at once that it would require two very good hits for them to reach it in the requisite number. Looking back, he saw a couple leaving the previous green and was immediately able to identify the four-square figure of Miss Pargeter, who was wearing a tweed skirt and green jumper. Even though he knew that at the very least she must be in her late seventies, having served in the war, she was striding purposefully ahead of her opponent, a much younger and slimmer woman, in fawn trousers and a matching shirt.

Sinclair positioned himself behind a convenient tree some distance behind the tee and watched the two of them as they approached.

'Right. All square and all to play for.'

Miss Pargeter took out her driver, lined up carefully and without much body turn and a modest backswing hit the ball mostly with her powerful forearms about 180 yards down the centre of the fairway. She then stood back and fixed her opponent with a gimlet eye as if to say 'take that'.

There obviously wasn't too much to go wrong with Miss Pargeter's conservative game, but one look at her opponent's practice swing told him that she was bound to be erratic – there was a looseness of grip at the top and, like a lot of women, she tended to overswing well past the horizontal. On this occasion, though, her timing was absolutely right and her ball, with a touch of draw on it, finished a good thirty yards ahead of the other one.

Roberta Pargeter's three wood finished some forty yards short of the green, but was again quite straight, whereas her opponent hit a low hook, also with a fairway wood, which bounced a couple of times before running through the greenside bunker and fetching up on the edge of the green. Sinclair saw Miss Pargeter shake her head and it didn't require any great expertise as a lip-reader to see that she mouthed the words 'Lucky sod!' Sinclair grinned to himself, already anticipating the drama ahead at the green and he wasn't disappointed.

Miss Pargeter pitched up to within six feet of the hole and the other woman putted to within four. If they both either holed out or missed, the match would have had to go on to extra holes but if either missed and the other holed, that one would be the victor, it was as simple as that. Sinclair correctly guessed the outcome as soon as Miss Pargeter had taken one quick look at the line, settled into her stance and with a firm rap sent the ball into the centre of the hole. Her opponent immediately began to prowl around, she studied the line from in front of the hole and then from behind, she looked at it from the side and then approached the ball as if it were surrounded by land-mines. Even after all that, she seemed unable to face hitting it and stood frozen, as if for an eternity, then gave it a sudden stab, missing the hole by a good six inches. To have said that the handshake that followed was perfunctory would have been an understatement and the detective would have been willing to bet that a few tears would be shed in the locker-room.

'Well played,' he said, coming up to Miss Pargeter as she walked towards the clubhouse.

The woman whirled round. 'So it was you skulking in the trees, was it?'

'Guilty – I couldn't resist the dénouement.'

'That woman's a much better golfer than me in a technical sense, but she's short of bottle – did you see her trying to settle to that putt? It wasn't a question of ants in her pants, more like bloody great termites. Ah well, another sworn enemy to add to the rapidly swelling list.'

'Why's that?'

'She's a bad loser and I'm a bad winner – a deadly combination, I'm sure you will agree. Enough of all that, how about that coffee? I somehow can't see your being tempted by anything stronger, on duty and all that. I'll just get out of these shoes and be with you in about five minutes.'

She was as good as her word and somewhat to Sinclair's surprise – he was expecting her to down a stiff gin – ordered a large pot for them both.

'Have one of these,' she said, lifting up the plate of assorted cakes. 'They're very good – home-made by the steward's wife.'

He contented himself with a small wedge of shortbread,

but she had no such inhibitions, demolishing a large Eccles cake and then lifting an equally impressive piece of fruit-slice on to her side plate.

'That's better. Now, you want to hear about Linda Baines, don't you?'

'I certainly do.'

The woman nodded. 'You really needed to see Linda and feel the force of her physical presence to understand what an effect she had on people. As well as being a wicked little minx, she had a sparkle about her and then there was that incredible body of hers. She hadn't reached or gone through the puppy-fat stage and her hips hadn't widened, either. You should have seen people's reactions when she did that streak last May, particularly that desiccated apology for a man, Cyril Atherton. He was umpiring and she capered about in front of him, then turned her back on him and did a spectacular handstand. I had my binoculars out and I can tell you, Cyril's eyes were neither raised to heaven, nor were they lowered to the ground, they were coming out on stalks, aimed at her perfect isosceles triangle.'

'Do you know Atherton well?'

'Pelton had him round to tea a few times and we see him at church, but I don't think anyone in the village knows him well. The mystery to me is why he ever came here in the first place. What is an ascetic missionary type doing in a cosy country town like Welbury? I could understand his staying for a while during convalescence from his illness, but he's been here now for twenty years.' She shook her head. 'What this place needs is a vicar with social skills, who is good with the young and at the same time appreciates the efforts of people like Pelton. She has done the flowers in the church for years without a word of

thanks or appreciation from Atherton. If it hadn't been for
Belling, who is very good at that sort of thing and who
frequently praises her to her face, or else writes her little
notes, she would have got discouraged ages ago.'

'I understand that Atherton runs a youth club.'

'He does indeed, but being Atherton he managed to
alienate people like Bert Stringer, who was very happy to
help and would have managed to instil some discipline
into the proceedings. After a bit, though, they all gave up
and the thing has become a shambles. On his own,
Atherton can't keep an eye on half of what goes on and I
gather that that half is quite interesting. These days, with
families being smaller, much less sport being organized in
schools, children being better fed and growing more
quickly, it's hardly surprising that things start to happen
when the sap begins to rise. Believe you me, it's not only
the young, either; lots of people in Welbury behave just as
wildly as Linda did – the only difference is that they aren't
so open about it.'

'How does Sir Geoffrey get on with Mr Atherton?'

'Well, like he gets on with everyone else. He's a good sort,
is Geoffrey, and if it hadn't been for him I think Cyril would
have gone berserk at that cricket match. No, I'm wrong, he
did go berserk; when Linda came down off her handstand
he turned to the stumps, pulled one out, and if Geoffrey,
who was umpiring at square leg the other end, hadn't
hurried up and restrained him, I'm quite sure he would
have set about her with it. He was beside himself with rage.'

'Is he normally like that?'

'Bad-tempered, you mean?' Sinclair nodded. 'He
certainly is. I reckon he's on a short fuse the whole time
and just occasionally there is an almighty explosion.
Cyril's problem, in my view, is chronic guilt.'

'Guilt? What about?'

'Sex. He is tortured by young girls. People are funny, aren't they? They fondly imagine that they're hiding their feelings and impulses and all the time they're shouting them to the skies. When they can't find anyone else, I play the harmonium at choir practices and poor old Cyril just can't control his eyes – that's the big give-away.'

'Do you think he ever tried anything on?'

'I doubt it very much. With Cyril it's all in the head and that's one of the reasons, I believe, that he was so shattered by what happened at the cricket match. Fantasies are one thing, but to be presented with the reality only six feet away from you and in public is quite another. After Linda had been bundled away I kept my glasses on Cyril and I could see that he was both as white as a sheet and literally shaking like a leaf. If it hadn't been for the tea-interval and Geoffrey taking him in hand, I don't think he would have been able to continue.'

'Belling sounds as if he's everyone's long-stop.'

'I met a lot of remarkable men during the war and so I know what I'm talking about when I say that Geoffrey Belling is one in a million. If I had been otherwise inclined, he would have been just the man I would have hoped to find. Nice is not a word I'm all that fond of, but I can't think of a better one to describe him. He's helpful to everyone in Welbury without being patronizing and manages to be excellent with young and old alike.'

'How did he get on with Linda?'

'According to Bert Stringer he was just about the only person she would listen to. Both he and Charles Crichton had a chat to her after that streak and it was Geoffrey who worked the trick. Although I've no idea what he said to her, he managed to get her to apologize to Bert and that must have been something of a record as far as she was concerned. Geoffrey was also marvellous with George Baines.

'George is a funny fellow; he was gentle and caring to Rose, as weak as water with Linda and yet at times he also has an explosive temper. He had a real go at Helen Crichton about a year ago in full view of quite a collection of interested bystanders. She came hurtling out of the courtyard of her house in the main street in reverse and had it not been for some very quick reactions on George's part, her car and Geoffrey's pride and joy, the Jaguar, would have had serious mischief done to them. By a happy chance, I was having a coffee in that small café right opposite and nipped out to watch the fun. He told her that she was a disgrace, that she shouldn't be on the road and that she ought to be breathalized.'

'What was her reaction to that?'

'She came out fighting like a fishwife. She wasn't prepared to take insolence from a mere servant, she would speak to Sir Geoffrey and have him dismissed, he was coming along the street far too fast, everyone knew that male drivers were aggressive and so on. If you ask me, she was lucky not to get a bunch of fives in the face.'

'How did Sir Geoffrey cope with that?'

'Predictably. He listened to what they both had to say, then interviewed a few witnesses and then got the two of them together. He told her that he was quite satisfied that George had been completely in the right and that she should apologize to him.'

'What did she say to that?'

'Geoffrey didn't tell me, merely that she had flung out in a rage, but after that, you can imagine that there hasn't been much love lost between them.'

'Does she drink?'

'Does she drink! The irony of it is that Margot Belling used to be her main partner in that particular crime.'

'Margot Belling?'

'Yes, didn't you know? Margot was Geoffrey's wife and she was killed in a car accident when she was over the limit. You can easily imagine, therefore, that he's more than a bit sensitive to drinking and driving, not to mention the fact that he's chairman of the local bench.'

'How does Dr Crichton react to his wife's drink problem?'

'Dignified silence. What else can the poor fellow do under the circumstances? Charles has had a rough time with Helen over the last few years and not only with the drink.'

'Oh, in what way?'

'The usual one. He got fed up with her, reacted by becoming a workaholic and she is said to have found consolation elsewhere, although that may just be a malicious rumour – Helen hasn't got many friends in Welbury. She'll have even fewer when it gets out that she has just had the trafficator cover on her Peugeot replaced.'

'What?'

'1 thought that might make you sit up. In fact, I only discovered it by accident; I was showing young Tim Forbes, our paper boy, my new Ford Fiesta and he said that it wasn't a patch on the new Peugeot. I jokingly replied that he didn't know what he was talking about and that I bet he'd never even been in one and he replied that his father, who is a mechanic at the garage up the road, which is a Peugeot agent, had taken him out on a road-test of Mrs Crichton's car and that it went like a bomb. I asked him what had been wrong with it, if it was such a marvellous car, and he then told me about the broken cover.'

'So you know about the bits of amber plastic on the road?'

'Yes. Fred Grimes and I saw them together.'

'That's all that Miss Pargeter had to say,' Sinclair said when the two detectives met the following morning at his office, 'and perhaps it was just as well that I wasn't able to spoil her moment of triumph; only after I got back here did I receive the same piece of information from the DC who was looking into it. He soon found that the plastic came from a Peugeot, he rang up the agents in the neighbourhood and it was as simple as that. That wasn't quite the end of the excitement for the day, either.' Sinclair opened the file and looked at Fiona across the desk . 'Dobson also had one or two surprises up his sleeve. He managed to do a very thorough job without letting Belling know what he had found; in fact, it was child's play – once he started to write down all the titles of the books, the man got bored and went downstairs to watch the golf on TV. You might care to take a look at the inventory he made.'

Sarah ran her finger down the neat columns, noting the quite considerable quantity of costume jewellery that the scene-of-crime man had found in the chest, protected by a layer of paper from the large collection of Lego in a cardboard box, some £300 in notes, hidden under the carpet near the wall at the side of her bed, and all the clothes, books, old toys and board-games in the chest.

'Notice anything funny?'

'The sheepskin jacket isn't listed.'

'Exactly.'

'Which presumably means that Belling gave it to Linda and doesn't want us to know.'

'Yes and my guess would be that he nipped up a ladder and through that open window after we had left to remove it, although I suppose he just might have found a spare key; Dobson told me that there was no evidence that the lock or the door had been tampered with. How did you get on with Dr Crichton?'

Sinclair listened intently as she gave an account of her meeting with the man and his wife.

'Good work,' he said when she had finished. 'What do make of it all, then?'

'Well, in view of all Linda's goings-on, I reckon we can be reasonably confident that the murderer was a local person.'

'I agree. What about Mrs Crichton, as a start?'

'She's obviously one of the prime suspects, but although she might have killed Linda by running her down in her car, I somehow don't see her having done so by hitting her on the head with a stone – I doubt if she would have had the strength, for one thing.'

'I don't know; it takes surprisingly little if the blow happens to land on a critical spot on the skull.'

Fiona nodded. 'It is true that she hated the girl, who she was convinced, rightly or wrongly, was having sex with her husband, and there is the evidence of her car, but if she is guilty, she would hardly have taken it to a local garage to be repaired, unless, of course, she reasoned that that is what everyone else would suppose.'

'You've met her; do you think she might have been as devious as that?'

'Very difficult to say. Certainly not in the state she was in yesterday when she had a lot of alcohol on board and was self-pitying and aggressive by turns.'

'I find it quite astonishing that she should have trotted out all that stuff about her marriage within minutes of having met you.'

'Drinkers are like that.'

It was said so definitely and with such feeling that Sinclair looked up and was just about to comment when he saw that she was flushed and biting her lip. He decided to let it pass.

'She at least seems to have been right about Linda being free with her favours,' he said after a pause, 'unless that girl Tracey was feeding you with some highly coloured fantasies.'

'It should be easy enough to prove one way or the other.'

'You mean by asking Rawlings to get to work with his DNA test on that young man?'

'Yes.'

'I think you're right; in this business it doesn't pay to take anything for granted. I think it would be a sensible thing to do. Perhaps you would see to it and also have a word with the young fellow, whatever his name is?'

'Phil Rouse.'

'That's the chap. As you were the one to talk to Tracey Farrell, you would also be the best person to tackle him, provided, of course, you feel happy about it. Do say if you'd like some support.'

'No, that's all right, thank you. I think I would be more likely to get him to talk on my own.'

'I agree. There's one last thing, if you've got time when you get back, I'd like you to see what you can dig up on that sheepskin jacket. By the way, should you need any ammunition in dealing with our friend Rawlings, you might care to take a look at the *Oxford Dictionary of Quotations*. There's a copy in the bookcase over there. Give me a ring later on, would you? Hope it all goes well. I'm just off to give Mr Watson a progress report. Incidentally, he's going to be on the news bulletins tonight – you might care to watch. Just pull the door to when you leave, would you?'

Fiona stood there for a moment after Sinclair had gone, a puzzled expression on her face. What on earth was he on about? He wasn't given to making irrelevant remarks and she supposed she had better try to look up the quotation, if only she could remember it. What was it that Rawlings had said? Wasn't it something to do with a steady hand? She flicked through the index, looking up 'steady' and found it straight away. 'Steady of heart and stout of hand'. Yes, that was it. Her eyes flicked up to the head of the page to look at the title of the work from which it had come and she shook her head in disbelief. God, she thought, how childish could you get? It was only when she thought about it later that she realized just how prissy and pompous she was being about it. It wasn't as if Rawlings had made the remark deliberately and when she thought about the forbidding Miss Ryle, she could see exactly why the pathologist had practically had an apoplectic fit. It was one thing, Fiona thought, on her way down to Welbury, to appear confident to Sinclair about tackling Phil Rouse, but it was quite another when there was the possibility of either bumping into George Baines, who made her distinctly uneasy, or Sir Geoffrey, who would undoubtedly want to know why she was so keen to see one of his employees.

After driving slowly past the lodge, which looked as if it was still shut up, Fiona found the lane which wound its way around the back of Belling's estate. She parked just out of sight of the wooden gates which guarded the entrance to a narrow road that was little more than a path. When she saw that it was overgrown with brambles and that there was a chain and padlock on the gate which clearly hadn't been opened for months, she climbed over. It was obvious when she had walked forward fifty yards or so that the land on which she was standing was part of the park attached to the Hall and that the farm was on the other side of the lane.

A short distance ahead of her there was a bank of rhododendrons on either side of the path; then the ground opened out and through the trees she could see the house with the lawn in front of it. To left and right there was a spectacular array of white, pink and blue hydrangeas. She was just admiring them when she saw a movement to her left. She retreated behind a large oak-tree. A very old man, his face very brown and weather-beaten under a battered felt hat, came walking stiffly and very slowly along the path, a wheelbarrow in front of him.

'Excuse me,' she said, 'could you tell me where I might find Phil Rouse?'

Fiona had often been told during her training that nervous and guilty people had a habit of saying too much. She had constantly to remind herself not to make the same mistake. The gardener's smile and the way he respectfully took off his hat was a clear indication that he saw nothing strange in a young woman in city clothes walking around Sir Geoffrey's garden.

''E's in the rose-garden, miss. It's behind that yew hedge yonder.' He pointed back the way from which he had just come.

After thanking him, Fiona waited until he had continued on his way. Then, keeping out of sight of the house, she walked briskly towards the hedge.

'Phil? Phil Rouse?'

The young man with the shock of fair hair, who had

been dead-heading the roses, turned round abruptly and coloured slightly as he turned to face her.

'Yes.'

'I'm Fiona Campbell,' she said, showing him her warrant card, 'and I'd like a word with you. Is there somewhere we could go and not be disturbed or overheard? How about the summer-house?' All the colour drained out of the young man's cheeks. 'Can you think of anywhere better?'

Head down, Rouse picked up his sweater which had been lying on the ground and turned. Fiona followed him through a gap in the hedge and along a path lined with shrubs. Some fifty yards further on they came to a grassy clearing at the back of which, half hidden by trees, was the summer-house. The door was locked, but she very quickly found the key on its hook under the eaves. Once they were seated on the cushions on the floor they were out of sight, well below the level of the windows.

'You did know that Linda Baines was under age, didn't you?'

'Under age?'

'Do you really need me to spell it out? She was fifteen and what you did with her on that Sunday was illegal.'

'It wasn't like that, it wasn't like that at all.'

'Tell me what it was like, then.'

The young man sat staring at the ground for a moment or two and then nodded.

'All right.'

'Hello, Phil.'

'Oh, hello Tracey.'

'You couldn't put the chain back on my bike, could you?'

Phil Rouse was getting more than a bit fed up with Tracey Farrell; she was always asking him to do this and that – if it wasn't fixing something she'd broken, it was helping her with her homework, or giving her a riding-lesson – but he was a kind-hearted young man, and didn't really mind that much, particularly as it gave him the chance to see Linda, who was often with her, and who had been constantly on his mind ever since the cricket match. He had never seen a girl of her age naked before, let alone one who had passed within ten feet of him when he had been fielding at long-leg and who had winked at him as she had run past. She was so pretty, so perfectly formed and so much more desirable in reality than she had been even in his wildest fantasies.

'Wakey, wakey!'

'I'm sorry, Tracey, I was miles away. Your bike, you said? Where is it?'

'Over there.'

He turned the machine upside down, resting it on its saddle and handlebars, and it was the work of a couple of minutes to thread the chain back on.

'There you are,' he said, turning the pedals with his hand and making the back wheel spin. 'The chain's got a bit loose – there are some tools in the shed over there and I'll tighten it up for you, if you like.'

'Thanks, Phil,' she said, when he had finished, 'you're a star. It's your birthday on Sunday, isn't it?'

'Yes.'

'Which one?'

'Nineteenth.'

She got on to her bike and began to circle him slowly.

'I've got a very special present for you.'

'What's that, then?'

'A surprise. I'll give it to you in the summer-house at half past three on Sunday.'

'Sounds exciting.'

'It is, it really is. You will come, won't you?'

'If you say so.'

'No, I'm not joking; I've gone to a lot of trouble over it.'

Phil Rouse very nearly didn't go; indeed, he had forgotten all about it until his mother, who was cooking him a special meal to have that evening when his father got back, shooed him out of the house.

'Why don't you take Gus for a walk?' she said. 'You can't spend the whole afternoon glued to the telly and it'll work your appetite up.'

Gus, an old Airedale, whose arthritic joints were troubling him, didn't want to go for a walk any more than Phil did. It was when he was trying to encourage the animal to move along just a bit faster that he remembered Tracey's invitation. It was probably just one of her practical jokes, he thought, but so what, he had nothing else to do.

He couldn't see anyone in the summer-house, but tied Gus to a tree with his long lead well away from it and knocked on the door.

'Come in.'

Linda, who had been sitting on one of the cushions on the floor, was just getting up as he went in. She stood there looking at him, a smile on her face.

'Happy birthday, Phil!'

Before he could move, she put her hands down and in one swift movement pulled her jumper over her head. He watched in disbelief as, without taking her eyes off his face, she began to unbutton her shirt. It couldn't be true, it just couldn't be happening, he thought, but then she began to ease her tight jeans down, her bra joined the pile of her other clothes and then she put her thumbs inside the waistband of her pants.

Close to, she was even more perfect than he had remembered from the cricket match and he stood there, aware that he was gawping at her like an idiot, but not knowing what to do. Linda put her forefinger to her lips, moistened the tip of it with her tongue and then began to run it down the length of her body.

'Come on, Phil, it's your turn now.'

If he had been asked about it beforehand he would have been forced to admit that he hadn't the first idea what to do, or how to do it, but there was no difficulty, no difficulty at all. Without seeming to be taking command, Linda nevertheless managed to indicate when she wanted him to speed up, when to slow down and when to move to somewhere new. Nothing he had heard or read about had prepared him for her warmth, her surprising strength and in the end, her total abandonment. The second time – he hadn't even known that there *was* a second time, having dismissed the tales at school as mere boasting and exaggeration – was slower, less urgent, gentler and every bit as satisfying.

Afterwards, though, had come the guilt and the fear, particularly the fear. Fear that he might have made her pregnant, that he might have picked up an infection, that Tracey would tell her friends what had happened and that his father or George Baines might find out. And if they did, would he be forced to marry her?

Phil Rouse was shaken to the core when, on returning home, he found that his father was already there, having come back unexpectedly early from Birmingham with Sir Geoffrey; suppose he had taken it into his head to take a stroll round the garden after his long drive? It didn't bear thinking about. That was only the start of it; supper that evening was a nightmare. His father was as taciturn and irritable as always, finding fault with everything; his mother, as anxious to please as ever, was in her customary state of anxiety and he couldn't get what had happened in the summer-house out of his mind.

'What's this?' his father said, pointing an accusing finger at the object on his plate.

'It's a clove.'

'Yes, I know it's a bloody clove and I can't stand them, as you very well know.'

'They do add to the taste of an apple pie, dear.'

The man let out a grunt of exasperation and turned towards his son.

'What's the matter with you, Phil?'

'I'm not hungry.'

'Your mother hasn't spent the whole afternoon cooking a special meal for your birthday for nothing. Give him a decent helping, Iris, and then, son, you'll bloody well eat it.'

'It doesn't matter, Ken, he can always have it tomorrow. Apple pie is just as good when cold, even better, in fact.'

When his father pushed his chair back and picked up the serving-spoon himself, Phil knew with utter certainty that if he was forced to eat one more mouthful, he would … The telephone rang in the hall and he clung to it like a life-raft, pushing his chair back and hurrying out to answer it.

'It's for you, Dad, Sir Geoffrey.'

When his father had left, shutting the door behind him, to Phil's astonishment, his mother spooned out the pie from his bowl, ate it in a matter of seconds and then handed it back empty, signalling him to put it on the place-mat in front of him. When his father came back she was just finishing what was left in her own bowl, but all the subterfuge was unnecessary.

'Linda Baines has been killed – raped and murdered.'

'I had nothing to do with it, you must believe me.'

Fiona began to pick idly at the wool on Phil's sweater, which was lying on the ground beside her.

'I do believe you, Phil, but I need to know exactly what you did after you left here and what time it was.'

'Well, Gus was asleep and as he often barks when he doesn't wake naturally, I decided to leave him there and sit for a while on the bench in the rose-garden. I remember looking at my watch and seeing that it was a few minutes after four-fifteen.'

'I think that Linda probably left on her bike by the rear entrance to the grounds not long after that and it's just possible that her killer followed her.'

'You mean that someone might have been watching the summer-house?'

Fiona nodded. 'You weren't all that far away, did you hear or see anything?'

Phil looked round at her for the first time since they had sat down.

'Gus started to bark not long after, and when I went to collect him I did see that some of the bracken quite near to him was trampled down.'

'Weren't you worried?'

'Not at the time. I thought it was probably Tracey.'

'Would you show me exactly where it was?'

She handed him his sweater and followed him out of the summer-house and between some trees.

'I tied Gus to this one here and the trampled-down area was over there.'

It had been dry ever since that Sunday and Fiona could still see quite clearly where someone had been standing. She was just about to walk away, when something caught her eye and she squatted down to look at it.

'Does Tracey smoke?'

'I think she has the odd one.'

Fiona picked up the cigarette-end with her handkerchief and put it into the plastic container in her bag.

'You won't tell my father about this, will you?'

'I certainly won't, but I'm afraid I can't promise that it won't come out.'

'It was Tracey who told you about me, wasn't it?'

'Yes, it was, but she has promised not to say a word to anyone about it and, if you value my advice, you won't either.'

After he had gone Fiona looked around the summer-house. Apart from the cushions on the floor and the pile of blankets, there were a couple of folding chairs, a radio-cassette player and a long wooden box with a faded label on it, indicating that at one time it had contained a croquet set. The badly rusted hasp was secured to the staple by a combination padlock and when she bent down to look at it more closely she saw that the studs holding the assembly in position were loose. By inserting her nail-file behind it, she was able to remove it and open the box. She lifted the two soft-porn magazines out, putting them to one side, together with the tins of cider and packets of chocolate biscuits, and then removed a cigarette from the single packet, which she also put in her bag. Finally, she inspected the two shoe-boxes, one of which contained a collection of cassettes and the other an object so out of place that she stood there looking at it for several minutes before resting it on the upturned end of the croquet box and photographing it from several angles. Only then did she replace all the objects and fix the hasp back on.

After locking up and replacing the key on its hook Fiona searched the undergrowth close to the place where the bracken had been trampled down. After a few minutes she found another cigarette-end; then, after taking a look through the knot-hole in the back of the summer-house, she went back to her car and drove slowly towards Welbury. Had Linda taken the same route and, if so, why? Had she gone to meet someone? The shortest way back to the lodge would have been in the opposite direction and after what she had been up to with Phil, surely, Fiona thought, the girl wouldn't have decided to go for an unnecessary cycle ride.

CHAPTER SEVEN

Fiona Campbell glanced in through the gates of the court-yard in front of the Crichtons' house as she drove past and saw something that had her braking sharply and turning into the car park by the side of the Green Man. She walked back and saw that the windscreen of Helen Crichton's car had been turned to sugar and that there was a gaping hole directly in front of the steering-wheel. Someone had also run a sharp instrument the whole way along the off-side, scoring the paintwork down to the underlying metal.

'Whatever happened to your wife's car?' Fiona asked Charles Crichton when he came out of his consulting-room to show a patient out.

'You'd better come in for a moment.'

He waved her to a chair, then lifted a brick out of the right-hand drawer of the desk.

'Someone heaved this through the windscreen of Helen's car last night and this was wrapped around it.'

He handed her a dirty sheet of paper on which had been pasted letters from a newspaper. YOU'LL DIE BEFORE YOU'RE SORRY she read out aloud, then looked up at the doctor 'Did you hear it happen?'

'No, my bedroom is on the other side of the house and

Helen was too deeply asleep to hear anything. She discovered it herself this morning.'

'Was she very upset?'

'Upset? She was hysterical. She straight away rang for a taxi, then rushed off without even saying goodbye properly, merely telling me that she was going up to London to stay in my brother's flat.'

'Where is that exactly?'

'In Maida Vale. He's in the States for three months and he left the key with us. Helen's been going up there each week to deal with the post and to make sure that everything's in order. I'll write down the address for you, if you like.'

'Thanks. Any idea who might have done it?'

'Not an inkling.'

'Do you know about the broken trafficator cover on your wife's car?'

'Yes, a "well-wisher" telephoned me about it last night.'

'What did your wife have to say about that?'

'She was asleep in her room when the call came through and this morning she was in no state to discuss anything.'

'Would you mind if I take the brick and the message? I would also like our men to examine your wife's car in detail; I'm afraid it will mean taking it away.'

'That's all right; I don't like it in the courtyard anyway. Helen should have moved it into the shed she uses as a garage last night, but she wasn't feeling up to it. It was when I asked her to do so this morning, that she discovered the damage.'

'I see. May I use your telephone, please?'

Charles Crichton nodded. 'Of course, but you'd better go into the house if you don't want to be overheard – you know the way, don't you? I must get on with the surgery.'

'Thank you. I won't trouble you again this morning, but I'll let you know at once if we discover anything.'

In the hall of the main part of the house Fiona stood for a moment in front of the telephone. Then, when she heard sounds from the kitchen, she ran lightly up the stairs. There were four bedrooms off the landing and, as Crichton had indicated, husband and wife clearly didn't share one of them. His was the single one facing away from the road. It was neat and tidy, everything being in its place, and his toilet accessories were all in the main bathroom, except for a pair of very elaborate ivory hair-brushes, with a silver shield set into the back of each of them. She picked them up and saw that they had been given to Crichton's father by his patients to mark his retirement.

Helen Crichton's room was the very reverse of neat; it was clearly the master bedroom with an *en suite* bathroom and it was equally obvious that neither she nor Hilda had cleaned it for several weeks. The bath was stained and greasy, the basin marked with blobs of solidified tooth-paste, the bed unmade and dirty underwear was scattered over the floor.

Hearing the sound of a vacuum cleaner from below, Fiona went back into Crichton's room and used the phone on the bedside table to contact the forensic people about the Peugeot. Then she dialled Rawlings's number. To her surprise, the pathologist himself answered rather than Miss Ryle.

'More specimens? My dear Miss Campbell, what an eager beaver you are, to be sure. Yes, one-thirty would suit me well. You might even care to join me in a post-prandial cup of coffee.'

Fiona managed to get away from the house without seeing anyone and set off for Rawlings's laboratory, having time beforehand for a snack at a nearby sandwich bar. The pathologist answered her knock himself.

'Ah, that's what I like to see – exactly on time, not a minute early, not a minute late. Are you one of nature's larks by any chance, Miss Campbell? You are? Just as I suspected; punctuality often goes with it. Quite unlike that owl of a woman, Miss Ryle; you may have noticed how irritable she was the other morning, like Count Dracula, she has a constitutional dislike of daylight.'

'Isn't she in today?'

'Had to take her old mother to hospital.'

'I thought she might be convalescing from the suggestion that she might be "The Lay of the Last Minstrel".'

Rawlings let out a great guffaw and slapped his thigh. '"Steady of heart and stout of hand", eh? A policewoman who knows her Scott? I don't believe it. But I was forgetting, you do come from north of the border.'

'I have to confess that I looked it up in the *Oxford Dictionary of Quotations*.'

'Did you, did you indeed? No, Miss Ryle is in blissful ignorance of that sobriquet and I rather think that it would be for the best if she were to remain so. She has many admirable qualities, but a highly developed sense of humour is not one of them. Now, what have you got for me?'

'Some specimens of hair.'

'Head, or body?'

'Head. I—'

'Don't tell me, I rather fancy a blind experiment and when I have the results for you, you can tell me how you came by them. I suppose you'd like the answers as soon as possible?'

'That would be very helpful.'

*

'Quite a lot else has happened today,' Fiona said, when she had explained to Sinclair on the telephone that Helen Crichton was in London.

'Hmm. In that case, I think we'd better see her tomorrow morning, even if it is a Saturday. Let me have your address and I'll pick you up at about ten, if that suits you.'

'Why not come in for a coffee before we leave? I'd like to show you what I found near the summer-house and the photos I took there.'

'Thank you, I'd like that.'

Fiona's flat was part of a conversion that had been done on a sizeable Victorian house and Sinclair was looking appreciatively round the living-room, with its high ceiling and elegant proportions when she came in with the coffee.

'Nice flat you've got.'

'Yes. I've been very lucky and it's all due to the generosity of my Auntie Ella. She had quite a big win on the lottery a year or two ago and wanted me to have some of it when it would be of most use, rather than waiting until later. It was that that allowed me to buy a car and make a substantial down-payment on the flat. It's got two bedrooms and now that I'm no longer sharing it with anybody it's really too big for me, but I like it and I've got used to living on my own and coming and going as I please, even though the mortgage is a bit of a strain.'

'Don't you get lonely?'

'Yes, I do at times, but I don't seem to be much good at living with other people. The job has something to do with that, not that I'm complaining.'

She had gone a bit pink and her normal slight Scottish

accent had become more pronounced. Sinclair decided to change the subject.

'Excellent coffee.'

'Colombian and one of my extravagances – I can't bear that canteen stuff.'

'That makes two of us. Now, tell me about that fellow Rouse.'

Fiona did so, clearly and concisely, mentioning that she had picked some hairs off his jumper and taken them to Rawlings.

'That's very satisfactory. What you found out from him tallies pretty well with Tracey Farrell's account.'

'I thought so, too, and I'm sure they hadn't got together to concoct the story, particularly as it doesn't reflect well on either of them.'

'Anything else?'

'Yes, there were two other things. I found these in an area near the summer-house where the undergrowth had been trampled down, not far from where Phil had tied up his dog.'

Sinclair opened up the handkerchief carefully and turned one of the two cigarette-butts over with his ball-point pen, bending forward to sniff it.

'Very interesting. And the other thing?'

'I had a look round the inside of the summer-house and took some snaps of the contents of an old croquet box.'

She gave him the photographs which she had had printed the previous afternoon.

'Good God!'

'It means something to you, then?'

'Indeed it does. I saw that figurine's non-identical twin on Roberta Pargeter's mantelpiece on Wednesday. I'm absolutely certain that they form a set together. Did you leave it in the summer-house?'

'Yes, I thought it better to do so.'

Sinclair nodded. 'I don't suppose you had time to check on that sheepskin jacket as well, did you?'

'Yes, I did and it didn't take long. Rochelle's is a very fancy boutique in Oxford which only stocks its own designer stuff.'

'And?'

'They sold several of those jackets just before Christmas and one was bought by credit card by none other than our friend—'

'Geoffrey Belling?'

'That's right, and the very snooty woman who runs the shop remembers the strikingly pretty girl who was with him at the time.'

'*Embarras de richesses*. Did Sir Geoffrey supply the money and other goodies as well, I wonder, and did Linda steal Miss Pargeter's figurine, or was she given it and what were those cigarette-butts doing near the summer-house?'

'And who messed up Helen Crichton's car?'

'Who, indeed? Shall we go?'

The flat to which Helen Crichton had moved was in the basement of a tall, Victorian terrace house in Maida Vale, no more than a quarter of a mile from Edgware Road. Being a Saturday, the area was deserted and Sinclair found a meter only a few yards away. The two detectives walked down the stone steps into the area at the base of them and when there was no reply to his ring, Sinclair peered through the thick metal bars protecting the window.

'See anything? Your eyes are better than mine.'

Fiona rubbed the glass with a tissue and got as close as she could.

'I think I can just make her out slumped in a chair.'

'Drunk?'

'I wouldn't be surprised.'

Sinclair set up a furious tattoo on the door. Just when he was wondering if he was going to have to do something dramatic such as kicking it in, Fiona told him that there was some movement from inside. The detective wrinkled his nose with distaste when Helen Crichton eventually opened the door; the woman was wearing a pink night-dress, the front of which was darkly stained, and the sour smell of vomit hung in the air. She looked at them vacantly, her mouth hanging open, then hiccuped loudly. If he hadn't put out a hand to steady her she would have fallen. He looked round the shambles that was clearly the living room and shook his head.

'See what you can do with her, will you, Fiona? I'll make a start at clearing up a bit in here.'

'Right. If you wouldn't mind looking after her for a minute or two, I'll see what the bathing facilities are like.'

'Good idea.'

The hot-water system hadn't been turned on, but at least there was a powerful shower over the bath, which had its own pump and electric heater. When she had mastered the controls Fiona went back into the living-room and, with Sinclair's assistance, put the woman, just as she was, into the bath.

'Sure you can manage?'

'Don't worry, I'm used to this sort of thing.'

'Give me a shout if you need any help.'

Fiona took off Helen Crichton's nightdress by the simple expedient of making a cut in it at the neckline with the nail-scissors she found in the glass-fronted cabinet above the basin and ripping it the whole way down the front. She looked at the woman as she lay with the back of her head resting on the end of the bath and shook her head. Helen Crichton was a mess. The fronts of her legs were bruised where she had blundered into the furniture, her hair was tangled, her nails broken and it didn't look as if she had had a good wash for several days.

Shouting at her and shaking her had no effect, but a blast of cold water from the nozzle of the shower certainly did. Her head jerked up, she looked around wildly and then she let out a stream of invective.

'Shut up!'

'Don't tell me to shut up, you fucking bitch.'

The ice-cold water took her full in the face and she began to cough and splutter, trying to get up, but Fiona held her down easily.

'I'm going to give you a good wash whether you like it or not and if you make things difficult there'll be plenty more where this came from.'

The needle-sharp jet of water hit the woman in the stomach and she let out a loud scream and then began to cry.

'That's better. Sit up, now. I said sit up.'

The woman flinched as Fiona raised the nozzle again and then pulled herself up, still sobbing bitterly. Forty-five minutes later, dressed in her brother-in-law's pyjamas and with her hair washed, dried and combed, she was hardly recognizable. A lot of her bite had come back, too.

'If you think you can barge in here,' she said to Sinclair, 'and allow that creature to assault me and that I'm going to sit down quietly under it, you have another think coming.' She took a couple of steps towards the telephone. 'I'm going to get on to my solicitor and then I'm ...'

'I think that would be a very good idea,' he said quietly. 'We can then all meet at Paddington Green Police Station and you will no doubt be able to explain how the near side trafficator of your Peugeot came to be broken and that some pieces of it were found on the road where Linda Baines was killed.'

'It was a plant,' the woman said wildly. 'I know what you police are like.'

'They were found by Miss Pargeter, long before we were involved in the case, and she'd make an impressive witness in court, don't you think? Look, why don't you sit down here quietly: we'll get you something to eat and then we can have a chat about it all. Is there any food here?'

The woman sank back into one of the easy-chairs and shook her head.

'I'll go and get some, then. Do you think you could eat something light such as scrambled egg?'

Sinclair took her lack of reaction to mean assent and after signalling to Fiona to stay with the woman, left the flat and walked up to the local shops.

'She's calmed down a lot now,' Fiona said after he had got back and they were both in the kitchen. 'She rang up just about her only friend in Welbury, a woman with whom she used to play tennis, who has agreed to put some of her clothes into a suitcase and I've promised to fetch it later today.'

'You don't want to do that, do you?'

'Not a lot, but in a way I feel sorry for her and at least she's more or less on our side at the moment and I don't want to lose that if it can be avoided.'

'You have a point there. Now, are you a dab hand with the eggs or shall I do my worst?'

Fiona laughed. 'You carry on; you're talking to one of the world's worst cooks.'

'That I find difficult to believe. Would you like some as well?'

'Yes, I would.'

It was quite the most extraordinary meal she had ever had, Fiona thought, as the three of them sat round the table in the living-room, eating the scrambled eggs, tomatoes, cheese and fruit that Sinclair had brought back. Helen Crichton wouldn't eat anything at first, but after she had been encouraged to drink a couple of glasses of lemon barley water, she did consent to tackle a small portion. By the finish she hadn't made too bad a meal. What was even more remarkable was that Sinclair managed to get her to talk about her physiotherapy training and she even became quite animated.

'Right,' he said when Fiona brought the coffee through. 'do you feel strong enough to tell us about that car of yours?'

'There's not much to tell. I found the broken plastic cover when I took it out on Monday and got it fixed straight away at Maggs's garage.'

'And you didn't go out in it at all on the previous day?'

'No, I didn't. It was parked in my garage.'

'Was it locked up?'

'No. About the one good thing you can say about Welbury is that people don't steal things. I always leave the key in the car and the garage isn't a proper garage at all; it's just an old shed at the bottom of the garden. It doesn't even have a door.'

'What about the Volvo?'

'Charles uses the genuine article off the courtyard, which is a lock-up.'

'Looking back on it, was there any evidence that your car had been driven by anyone else?'

'How do you mean?'

'The driver's seat in a different position, for example, or you might have noticed that it wasn't parked in exactly the same place in the shed.'

Helen Crichton thought for a moment. 'No, I can't say there was. I like the seat very upright and quite near to the steering-wheel and it was like that when I took it to Maggs's place; I noticed at once that it had been moved when I went to pick it up again.'

'What about its position in the shed?'

'I like to reverse it in, because the turn out on to the road is more than a bit tricky, being rather blind, so ...' She suddenly looked up. 'I'm not drunk now, neither am I a complete idiot, so I know what you're getting at. It would have been convenient for me, to say the least, if someone else had taken it out, but I don't think they did.'

'Does your husband ever drive the Peugeot?'

'What, with a backside like his? He can't even get into the seats properly, let alone squeeze himself through the door when it's in the shed. It's a pretty tight fit even for me, and you've seen how thin I am.'

'Why didn't you park in the shed on Thursday night? I gather that your car was in the courtyard when that brick was thrown through the windscreen.'

'If you must know, I had been drowning my sorrows and I was incapable of taking it out on the road, even for that short distance.'

'We think that Linda was killed at around five o'clock last Sunday, give or take half an hour or so. Would you mind telling me where you were between those times?'

'I was with someone, if you must know.'

'A man?' Helen Crichton nodded. 'Are you prepared to tell me his name?'

'You don't believe me, do you?'

'You're in trouble, Mrs Crichton. Someone in Welbury obviously thinks that you killed Linda and I've seen weaker evidence than that broken trafficator cover on your car lead to the conviction of someone, but if you have an alibi, say from between four and six that day, then it would be quite another matter.'

The woman hesitated a long time before replying. 'It was a man called Alec Earnshaw and if you must know, we were in one of his disused barns. Sordid, isn't it?'

'Were Sundays a regular fixture?'

'That's hardly what I would call it – you make it sound like one of Charles's beloved matches at Twickers – but yes, it was.'

'What about tomorrow?'

'I gave him a ring when I got here to put it off.'

'Do you mind if I have a word with him?'

'No, but he won't admit it, you know. Would you in his place? He's married and Virginia wouldn't like it, she wouldn't like it at all. She's strait-laced and one of the once a week with the lights out brigade and even then, only if he insists, which he doesn't nowadays. Alec and I go in for rather more sophisticated exercise, so perhaps "fixture" isn't such a bad word after all. Anyway, Alec has children and a place in the community and being found out by his wife is definitely not on the agenda.'

'Where exactly is this barn of his?'

'You don't want me to draw a map, do you?'

Sinclair ignored her sarcastic tone completely. 'That would be most helpful.'

'What about a sketch to illustrate what we were doing last Sunday?'

The detective allowed himself the suspicion of a smile. 'I don't think that will be necessary. There's no reason why your husband should know about your alibi, either. We have the useful phrase of "so-and-so being dismissed from our enquiries."'

Helen Crichton pressed her lips together. 'I was about to say that he wouldn't care even if he did find out, but that wouldn't be true. He can be very jealous, can Charles, and he can't always control himself when he loses his temper.'

Sinclair looked at his watch. 'We've got to go now; one of us will keep in touch with you and Fiona will bring you some more clothes later today. Is there anyone you can stay with over the weekend?'

'If you're worried that I'm going to drink myself silly again, you can relax. I cleaned Paul's drink cabinet out last night and I haven't got much money with me. Anyway, I haven't any friends in London now and I'm not going back to Welbury.'

Fiona waited until late in the evening before ringing Sinclair at his house. 'How did you find her when you went back with her clothes?' he asked.

'As good as I've seen her – she'd even done quite a reasonable job of cleaning the flat up.'

'What I can't understand is how she managed to recover so quickly this morning.'

'I'm sure that a lot of her trouble was due to dehydration – drunks perk up amazingly quickly when you correct it and she told me this afternoon that she hadn't taken in any liquid at all since the previous evening after she passed out, having finished a whole bottle of gin.'

'That would have put me in a coma for a week.'

'Really heavy drinkers can develop quite an amazing tolerance until their livers are shot to pieces.'

'The question is will she be able to keep off the stuff and was she telling the truth about her lack of money?'

'I think she was. There's no doubt that she's absolutely terrified as the result of that attack on her car and she made me promise not to tell anyone where she was; she also said that she had pleaded with her husband not to either. The one good thing about this is that it seems to have given her a real jolt and the realization that she can't carry on the way she's been doing.'

'I hope you're right. Would you feel strong enough to come down to Welbury again with me tomorrow afternoon? I ought to see this Earnshaw character and perhaps you'd take a look at the barn.'

'All right.'

'Good. I'll pick you up at your flat at about three.'

The following morning Fiona couldn't get the thought of Helen Crichton out of her mind. She decided to see how she was getting on before going to meet Sinclair. The woman's response was hardly encouraging.

'What the hell do you want, now?' she said.

'I just wanted to make sure that you were all right.'

'Did you think I was going to do a bunk? Kill myself, even?'

'No, but I was concerned about you.'

'I'll believe that when they supply gin on the National Health Service.'

'It happens to be true.'

Helen Crichton looked at her for a moment, then her chin began to tremble and she burst into tears.

'I'm sorry.' she said, when she had recovered. 'I didn't

mean to be so rude. I'm frightened and there's no one I can talk to. You do believe that I didn't kill Linda, don't you?'

'Yes, I do, but we still need evidence to support what you told us – you do understand that, don't you?'

'I really was with Alec last Sunday, you know.' She shook her head. 'I don't know why I go on seeing him. The sex was exciting for a time, but even that began to pall recently and, apart from that, I don't even like him. In his way, though, I suppose he cares for me and that's more than anyone else does.'

'Why don't you get a job when all this is over?'

'Charles wouldn't let me.'

'Surely you can't mean that.'

'You don't know my husband. Alec wasn't the first and Charles found out about it. Our marriage had already begun to develop cracks and he made it quite clear that if I wanted to stay with him there were certain conditions.'

'And what were they?'

'Discretion over any affairs – we had long since given up sharing a bedroom – not working, and doing my stuff at local events.'

'Why didn't you leave him?'

'No money of my own. My father still gives me a generous allowance, but he's one of those people who think that if you're married, you stay married, and he made it quite clear that if I ever left Charles it would stop and there would be nothing for me in his will, either. You're no doubt thinking that I would have been better off leaving despite that and maybe you're right. Anyway, I didn't, I got bored, began to drink and the rest just happened.'

'Did you really mean it when you told me about your suspicions of your husband and Linda?'

'To be honest, I don't believe that Charles can get it up at all these days and it wasn't even true about his giving her a feel. It was a spiteful thing to have said and I'm bitterly ashamed of myself now.'

'Can you think of anyone who might have tried to set you up?'

The woman shrugged her shoulders. 'Welbury is a small place and I'm well known there. I don't suffer from the delusion that my drinking habits are a secret and any number of people would know about it and that my car is kept in that shed. Anyway, it's clearly visible from the street.'

'What about the damage to your car?'

'There are lots of people there who would enjoy putting the boot in once the rumours started to fly around – I've made plenty of enemies over the years.'

When Fiona got up to go Helen Crichton saw her to the door.

'Miss Campbell,' she called out as Fiona began to climb the stone steps.

'Yes.'

'Thanks. It was very nice of you to look in to see me – I appreciate it very much.'

CHAPTER EIGHT

The long dry spell had ended and large drops of rain were beginning to fall as Sinclair brought his car to a halt a few yards short of the signpost which indicated the turn to Brook Farm.

'If Helen Crichton's map is accurate the barn should be through that wood we passed a hundred yards or so back. Why don't I pick you up on the road there, say in about an hour's time, or before, if I don't get anywhere with our friend Earnshaw? You'd better take my umbrella – it's on the shelf behind the back seat.'

The lane leading to Brook Farm was quite narrow and Sinclair was only half-way along it when a man, who was wearing a tweed cap, a knee-length, dark-green anorak and Wellington boots and who was walking towards him, held up his hand imperiously.

'Didn't you see the sign? This road only leads to my farm,' he said aggressively as Sinclair wound down the window.

'I did indeed. You must be Alec Earnshaw.'

'What if I am?'

The detective held out his warrant card. 'Inspector Sinclair. I'd like a word with you, if I may.'

'What about?'

'Linda Baines's death.'

'Linda Baines?'

'Yes. Do you think we might have a chat up at your house?'

'I don't wish my family to be disturbed on a Sunday afternoon. If you care to back up the lane, I'll show you where you can park along the main road.'

The man walked past the car, signalling to Sinclair to follow him. The detective reversed back the way he had come. There was a wooden gate leading to a field about fifty yards beyond the turning to the farm, and when Sinclair had pulled off the main road beside it Earnshaw got in the passenger seat.

'As I'm sure you know by now,' Sinclair said, 'Linda Baines was killed last Sunday, and small country towns being small country towns, I am equally sure you know that Mrs Crichton is suspected of having been responsible by knocking her off her bicycle with her car.'

'And what does that have to do with me?'

'Linda died at some time between four and six on that afternoon and Mrs Crichton says she was with you then.'

'With me? Doing what?'

'What men and women often do in private together.'

'Inspector, is this some sort of joke? Have you seen Helen Crichton?'

'Indeed I have.'

'Then you'll know that she drinks like a fish and quite frankly, if I wanted to have a fling, which as a happily married family man I certainly do not, then Helen Crichton is one of the last people I would select. If one wanted to be charitable, one would say that she was an inveterate romancer and if not, that she's a pathological liar. I feel sorry for her in a way – everyone knows that she and Charles don't get on.'

'Why is that?'

'Charles is a very worthy fellow, but he is a bit dull and Helen, before she took to the drink, was vivacious and most attractive. A place like Welbury was quite wrong for her; what she needed were the bright lights and some excitement.'

'Do you know them well?'

'We used to be very friendly with them at one time, bridge and that sort of thing, but there were one or two unpleasant scenes between the two of them, which upset my wife; our visits to each others' houses grew less frequent and eventually stopped altogether.'

'Is Charles Crichton your doctor?'

'No. We've always had Nicholson – I don't believe in having a GP who is a personal friend. Charles and I still play golf together occasionally.'

'May I ask what you were doing last Sunday between four and six?'

'I was working on one of my tractors – I've always done my own maintenance.'

'Anyone able to back you up on that?'

'Only my wife, who had something to say about the state of my hands and clothes when I came in.'

'Why do you suppose Mrs Crichton made up that story about you?'

'It's difficult to answer that without appearing conceited, but the truth of the matter is that she's fancied me ever since she came here. To be honest, it's been a considerable embarrassment to me and even more to my wife. I'm not denying that she was very attractive twenty years ago, but more recently – well, you've seen her yourself.'

Sinclair turned the car. As he drove back down the road

he waved at the man and in the wing mirror saw him still standing there until he rounded the bend and Earnshaw disappeared from view. He brought the Ford to a halt some distance further on, well away from Earnshaw's land, then walked back to the spot where he had agreed to meet Fiona. He had quite a long wait and was on the point of going to look for her when she appeared through the trees.

'Sorry I was so long – I very nearly got caught by our friend, the farmer.'

'Did you now? In that case, I don't think it would be a bad idea to get well clear of this place.'

'You know something,' Sinclair said when he had parked on the outskirts of Welbury, 'I was quite impressed by that fellow Earnshaw and when I was with him I thought he was probably telling the truth.'

'I suppose he denied having anything to do with Helen Crichton.'

'Yes, he did, but it was done quite subtly. He didn't deny that she had been attractive when younger and that she had made something of a set for him, but his line was: "you've seen her, would a man like me, if he'd wanted to have an affair, the very idea of which is absurd with such a lovely wife and family, really have selected an alcoholic ruin like Helen Crichton?" I thought he had a point; he is both well-preserved and good-looking.'

'And what made you change your mind?'

'The expression on your face when you said that he had nearly caught you and the fact that he was at the barn. You discovered something there, didn't you? Come on, out with it?'

Fiona laughed. 'I always knew I'd never make a poker-player.'

*

The barn was half-hidden by the surrounding trees and Fiona picked her way carefully through the undergrowth, standing just inside the entrance and waiting for her eyes to adapt to the gloom. After a minute or two, she was able to make out the large pile of sacking in one corner, the rusted remains of a bicycle and some ancient farm machinery and the fact that there was a loft, the entrance to which was by a trap-door. She was about to move further in when she heard the creak of a board from above. She froze immediately, her heart thumping, and then inched her way backwards, looking up and listening intently. A further two to three minutes went by, then she heard it again, followed by a half-suppressed giggle. Fiona stepped into the centre of the barn, picked up a long-handled rake and thumped the ceiling with it.

'Police! Come on, open up. I know you're there and I want to have a word with you.' When there was no response, she called up again. 'If you don't come down, I'll get my colleague outside to fetch Mr Earnshaw.'

There was another long pause, but when she turned towards the entrance she heard a series of noises from the loft, the trap-door was opened and then the end of a wooden ladder appeared through the rectangular hole in the ceiling. Before the two boys could come down Fiona started up the ladder and the smaller of the two, a cheeky-looking lad with ginger hair, who couldn't have been more than eleven or twelve, held out his hand to pull her up.

'You're not really from the police, are you?'

'Yes, I am. Ever seen one of these?'

The boy squinted at the warrant card and then gave it back.

'We weren't doin' no 'arm, miss. It's our lair, in't it Tom?'

'Seems pretty snug to me.' Fiona looked round at the packets of crisps, the soft-drink cans and the cassette player. 'Do you come here often?'

The ginger-haired boy shook his head. 'We only just fahnd it, didn't we, Tom?'

'You were here last Sunday, weren't you?'

'No, we wasn't. We didn't see nothing, honest.'

'Oh yes you did.' She turned to the other boy, who was doing his best not to burst into tears. 'Tell me what you saw and I promise that you won't get into trouble. Come on, let's pull up the ladder and close the trap-door, so that no one will disturb us.'

They still showed some reluctance to talk, but once Fiona threatened to march them up to the farm and leave Earnshaw to deal with them, they soon changed their minds.

They had found the barn a couple of months earlier when they were out on their bicycles and there had been a sudden downpour. They had sheltered under the trees, started to explore when they got bored with waiting for the rain to stop and there it was. They had even found an old ladder leaning against one of the walls, which gave them access to the loft through the trap-door. The fact that several of the rungs were broken and that the wood was rotten in places didn't worry them at all – it added to the sense of adventure. It was just what they had always wanted; a private place with no one to nag them, where they could eat crisps and sweets to their hearts' content, imagine that they were astronauts on their way to Mars and listen to their cassettes.

To start with, they were very careful not to make a noise,

but when they had paid several visits and it was obvious that no one ever came near they began to relax, and if it hadn't been for the man knocking over a scythe one Sunday afternoon, they might well have been caught. Through a large gap between two of the floorboards, they saw him open the large suitcase, glance through the contents and then close it again before going out. They waited for nearly ten minutes, not daring to move and then a woman came in, changed into a nurse's uniform from the suitcase and laid out the blanket and pillow on the floor, on which the man, now dressed in pyjamas lay down.

'What happened then?'

'They did rude things.'

Sinclair shook his head. 'Good God! And there's no doubt that it was Earnshaw and Helen Crichton?'

'None at all, particularly from their description of a natural redhead, although the boys didn't put it quite like that, and a tall man with a moustache. Anyway, I saw him when I was still with the boys; he came into the barn wearing a flat cap and an anorak and thank the Lord we heard him approach.'

'What did he do?'

'Just looked around suspiciously for a few minutes and then went off again. I thought it wise to wait for a good quarter of an hour before leaving – he looked a bit of a dodgy customer to me. The boys obviously thought so, too, and weren't coming down until they were quite sure that the coast was clear.'

'And they were there last Sunday?'

'They certainly were and, reading between the lines, it was something of a command performance – a priest applying penance to a wayward nun that time seems to have been the main course. I thought Helen Crichton's bruises were due to her having fallen about in the flat while drunk, but that doesn't appear to have applied to the ones on her backside.'

'I see. Well, it certainly sounds as if those two's fun and games occupied most of the time between four and six.'

'Yes, I gather so. The two of them evidently fell asleep after their exertions and the boys were late back home for their evening meal as a result.'

'Did you get their names and addresses?'

Fiona nodded. 'I doubt if they would have made them up, but even if they did, there can't be all that many schools in that area and if need be, we could find them in that way.'

'How do you suppose Helen Crichton got to the barn if she didn't use her car?'

'On foot, I imagine. It can't be more than half an hour's walk from the village.'

'That's true. Well, if those boys weren't telling you a pack of lies, and it all seems to hang together, Helen Crichton seems to be in the clear and it makes that broken trafficator cover on her car even more intriguing. It looks to me as if Linda Baines wasn't knocked off her bicycle by a car after all, and if she was, not by the Peugeot, which means that the murderer must have broken the plastic in that shed and then taken the pieces back to the scene of the crime.'

'Which is an extraordinarily calculated thing to have done after having just killed someone.'

'It certainly is. By the way, while we're down here, and in view of that figurine you found in the summer-house, I think that another visit to Miss Pargeter might be rewarding. If nothing else, I'd like you to meet her.'

In answer to the detective's ring Amelia Pelton came to the door.

'I'm afraid that Roberta won't be back until quite late, Inspector,' she said after Sinclair had made the introductions. 'She's playing in a match at Stoke Poges today.'

'That's all right. In fact, you were the one I wanted to see, Miss Pelton.'

'Me?'

'Yes. Mr Baines told me that Linda used to help you in the garden sometimes and I am interested in your impression of her. May we come in?'

'I'm so sorry, of course you may and why don't I put the kettle on? I'm sure you could do with a nice cup of tea on a horrid day like this.'

'That would be more than welcome.'

'Good. You know your way into the sitting-room, don't you?'

While the woman was in the kitchen Sinclair pointed to the porcelain shepherd-boy on the mantelpiece. Fiona picked it up and examined it carefully.

'As you said, they must surely be a pair. Did you really want to talk to Miss Pelton?'

'Not specially, but it wouldn't do to let her think so and she may come up with some tit-bits of information, you never know.'

Sinclair prowled round the room, looking at the books, until he heard the sound of the trolley outside and went to the door.

'My goodness,' he said, helping the woman in with it, 'this takes me back. I haven't seen such a marvellous tea-set since my old aunt died. Look, Fiona, have you ever come across a hot-water pot like this before? Do you see? It rocks in its cradle for pouring and has a spirit-lamp underneath to keep it warm.'

That wasn't all of it, either, the teapot was also silver, as was the milk-jug and the container for the toasted muffins.

'I was admiring that Meissen figurine on the mantel-piece,' said Sinclair when he had finished his cup of tea. 'You really do have some lovely things here.' He got up to look at it again. 'Surely it was one of a pair at one time, wasn't it?'

'That's quite right, it was. It upset us both so much when the other one was broken a few weeks ago – the pair had particular sentimental value, as I gave them to Roberta for her seventieth birthday some years ago.'

'What a tragedy! How did it happen?'

'One of those stupid things. Roberta took it down to dust, the telephone went, she put it down on that occasional table over there and while she was out of the room, Louis must have knocked it over with his tail.'

'And it couldn't be repaired?'

'No. Roberta told me that it was completely shattered and that there wasn't a hope of doing anything about it.'

'So you weren't here at the time.'

'No. I was down at the church doing the flowers and she thought it would cause me less distress if I didn't see the remains – Roberta is very thoughtful like that. Mr Atherton was also most sympathetic, too, when I told him about it. He had admired them so much when he came to tea one day. Don't tell her, will you, but I managed to find a replacement and I'm going to give it to her for her next birthday in a few weeks' time. The shop I bought the original from in Reading had closed and so I asked Mr Atherton, who knows a lot about *objets d'art*, and he put me on to a place in London.'

'How splendid! I'm sure she'll be absolutely delighted.'

'I certainly hope so.'

'Now, what about Linda Baines?'

'I can't be a great deal of help, I'm afraid. Roberta thought I needed some assistance in the garden – it's true, it had been getting a bit much for me – and she asked Sir Geoffrey if he knew of anyone. It was he who suggested Linda and I thought she was a very nice girl; she did a lot of the rough work and was willing and cheerful. It was lovely for me, too, to have someone young to chat to for a change. She told me all about her athletics, which I found most interesting. You may not believe it, looking at me now, but I was quite good at games when I was in India after the war and I often wish that I'd had the opportunities that young people have nowadays. We talked about other things as well – she used to love looking at my old photo-albums – and it's funny that we should have been talking about the figurines – Linda was most taken with them, particularly the shepherd girl, the one that got broken.'

'Did she work for you right up until the time of her death?'

'No. Roberta dismissed her about three weeks ago.'

'Really? What for?'

'Said she'd been rude and insolent to her. To be honest, Roberta can be very abrupt and intolerant at times and I expect Linda just answered her back – she wasn't in the least overawed by her. Anyway, it was a terrible shock for Roberta to have found the girl dead like that and I was most upset myself – Linda was so full of life.'

'Did she ever chat to you about her personal life? Boyfriends, for example?'

'We never got round to discussing that. I'm afraid that I did most of the talking – Linda seemed fascinated to hear about my experiences in the war in Burma and India. She very much wanted to travel herself and told me she was saving up for a trip to Australia. Poor Linda! The real world can't have been easy for her and she had her dreams – don't we all?'

'We do indeed.' The detective glanced at his watch. 'We really ought to be going. Thank you so much for the tea – I always did think that it was the most civilized of meals and it's a great pity that people no longer seem to have time for it or take it seriously.'

'I enjoyed seeing you both very much.'

Sinclair glanced across at Fiona as he fastened his seat-belt.

'You looked very preoccupied in there; anything on your mind?'

'Yes, that figurine in the summer-house.'

'And what it would do to Miss Pelton if it saw the light of day?' Fiona nodded. 'The same thought had crossed my mind. I'd like to see the set-up around that summer-house now, unless you're in a tearing hurry.'

'No, I'm not doing anything for the rest of the day.'

'Good. Now, how do I get on to that road that runs behind the Hall?'

Light rain was still falling as they climbed over the padlocked gate.

'Linda must have followed the same route as us in reverse when she left,' Fiona said as they approached the summer-house, 'and it was just over here that Phil Rouse tied up his dog and I found those cigarette-ends.'

Sinclair walked around the area for a few minutes, inspecting both the ground and the exterior of the hut.

'And Tracey was looking through here, was she?' he asked, pointing to the loose knot of wood.

'That's right. Would you like me to open up?'

Sinclair nodded and watched as Fiona reached up for

the key, unlocked the door and pulled the croquet-box away from the wall.

'That's funny,' she said. 'I remember pressing these loose studs in quite firmly and this one's half out.'

'Are you quite sure?'

'Absolutely.'

'I see. In that case, if what I suspect has happened, has, in fact, happened, then we'll have to be careful about any prints. It looks like no peace for Dobson.'

Using his handkerchief, the detective carefully pulled off the hasp, lifted the lid and looked inside.

'Anything missing?'

'Yes, the most lurid of the magazines and, more important, one of the shoe-boxes as well.'

'And with it, no doubt, the figurine.' When he opened the second box and saw the collection of cassettes, he straightened up and frowned. 'The only good thing about this is that it saves us having to make a decision about what to do with the wretched thing. Who do you reckon took it?'

'Miss Pargeter?'

'My money would be on Belling. He must have been the one to remove the coat from Linda's room and if he had been showering her with gifts, he might well have decided to take a look in here.'

'Do you think he killed her?'

'Because she was blackmailing him? It's certainly possible and a further word with him now wouldn't come amiss.'

Belling came out into the hall when his housekeeper had announced their arrival.

'As we were passing, I thought we would look in to report progress,' Sinclair said when they were sitting in the study.

'That's very good of you.'

'We've been able to establish that Linda was in your summer-house with Tracey Farrell not long before she was killed. She had left her bicycle just outside the back gate and we think that she must have gone to the village on it, before starting back for home. Now, it can't have escaped your notice that there was a very expensive hi-fi set in Linda's bedroom and our man also found some costume jewellery and quite a lot of money. From what little her father was able to give her and from what she earned from you and Miss Pargeter she would never have been able to accumulate all that, which leads one to the conclusion that she was given them, either voluntarily or as the result of some pressure.'

'You mean she might have been blackmailing somebody?'

'That's certainly possible, or, as I said, they might have been gifts. Did you give them to her, Sir Geoffrey?'

'What do you mean?'

'You did buy her a sheepskin coat for over five hundred pounds at a boutique by the name of Rochelle in Oxford and if you did that, it seems not unreasonable to wonder if you gave her the rest as well.'

Belling fiddled with the packet of cigarettes on his desk and then looked up.

'Linda was my goddaughter and I gave it to her for Christmas. I saw it advertised in a magazine, thought it would be a nice idea and we went to Oxford together to select it. She had never had much in the way of really good things and was thrilled to bits. I'm quite sure she had no idea that it was quite so expensive.'

'Why did you remove it from her room?'

'I thought it a bit strange that Linda should have kept

her room locked and when you had gone I decided to see if I could open it with one of the selection of old keys I keep in my workroom. I suppose you could put it down to idle curiosity. Anyway, I found one that fitted and noticed at once the hi-fi set and the suede handbag. I reckon that I can put two and two together as well as the next man and I thought that my present to her might be misinterpreted, so I removed it – it was a very stupid thing to have done.'

'Did you give her anything else?'

'I have always given her reasonably generous presents for Christmas and her birthday.'

'Such as?'

'Toys and books when she was younger, then money and a pair of leather boots for her last birthday.'

'How much money?'

'Usually twenty-five pounds. I thought that any more might embarrass George.'

'Did he know about the coat?'

'Of course.'

'And you didn't give her the hi-fi set, the bag or any jewellery?'

'No, I didn't.'

'Tell me about the summer-house.'

'I let Linda and Tracey Farrell use it as a den and the only time I went near it was when they invited me to tea there one day. You know what young people are like – they need a bit of privacy – and I'm sure that they wouldn't have wanted me snooping around. I know I wouldn't have at their age. Adolescents do funny things at times and it doesn't do to catch them at it. It makes one have to react and that isn't always in everyone's interests.'

'What were you doing that Sunday afternoon between four and six?'

'Let me think, now. I got back from Birmingham with Rouse at about three-thirty and I went for a stroll in the grounds to get some fresh air. After that, I came back here for a cup of tea and then watched the cricket on TV.'

'Who were playing?'

'Surrey and Notts.'

'Did you see anyone in the grounds?'

'Only Phil Rouse taking his dog for a walk, but I'm pretty certain he didn't see me.'

'Did your housekeeper get tea for you?'

'No, she was out for the day. I wasn't expecting to be back until later.'

'And you haven't been to the summer-house since Linda's death?'

'No, I've had no reason to.'

'Would you mind if I got my man, Dobson, to take a look at it?'

'The same fellows who came to the lodge?'

'That's right.'

'No, of course not.'

In the rear-view mirror of his car Sinclair saw Belling looking after them until they went out of sight round the bend in the drive.

'Did you think he was telling the truth?' Fiona asked as they turned into the road.

'I'm not sure. It's interesting that he left Dobson to his own devices at the lodge and he didn't seemed worried about the summer-house, but he's a pretty cool customer, is Belling, and did you notice that he failed to ask us how we knew about that coat?'

'Yes, I did and he must also have realized that we had also been in Linda's room that morning.'

'I doubt, though, if he removed that figurine from the

summer-house; surely, if he had, he would have reacted more to my asking permission for Dobson to give the place the once over.'

'Belling obviously smokes; were his cigarettes the right ones for those stubs?'

'I'm not enough of an expert to be able to tell.'

Sinclair drew up his car outside her flat and as Fiona started to undo her safety belt he turned towards her. 'Look, you've done most of the hard work up to now, why not take tomorrow off? You deserve it and a break never did anyone any harm. In any case, I've got to report to Watson tomorrow and there's the press conference on Tuesday morning. Why don't we meet after that, say at about twelve in my office? By then we'll have Dobson's report on the summer-house and the forensic lab may have come up with something on those cigarette-stubs.'

CHAPTER NINE

'You do spoil me, Pelton – I don't know what I'd do without you.'

Roberta Pargeter looked at the fluffy mound of scrambled egg on its neat square of toast, the two crisp rashers of bacon and the two large halves of tomato for a few moments with eager anticipation, then picked up her knife and fork.

'You need a decent meal before your golf, particularly on a windy day like this.'

'I certainly do and you'll see, the miserable grapefruit, dry toast and herbal tea brigade will start to flag half-way through the round, but not yours truly. This is what I call a breakfast!'

Amelia Pelton flushed with pleasure as she watched her friend wipe her lips vigorously with her napkin and then cover the slice of toast with thick layers of butter and marmalade. She did worry about Roberta's diet at times – the word cholesterol seemed to jump out at her every time she opened a newspaper or magazine – but she had to admit that her friend seemed immune to its ravages. Even though her next birthday would be her seventy-ninth, she never ailed with anything, not even a cold, and her energy and vitality seemed totally undiminished.

'Would you like another cup of coffee, Roberta?'

'I'm tempted, Pelton, sorely tempted, but I'm already beginning to get a touch of the yips on the putting-green and I doubt if an extra dose of the dreaded caffeine will help that dire affliction. Here, I'll give you a hand with the washing-up before I go.'

'That's all right – you'll want to be getting on your way.'

'Are you quite sure?'

'Off you go. Play well and drive carefully.'

'Since when did I do otherwise, you old fusspot?' Roberta Pargeter came across the room to her friend and lifted up her chin. 'You look tired. You're not to go over-doing it in the garden, do you hear?'

'Perhaps I will give it a miss this morning.'

'Very sensible. Don't wait for lunch – I'll have something at the club. Come on, Louis. Don't just stand there, you stupid animal.'

Amelia Pelton watched as the Labrador ambled after his mistress, wagging his tail, and soon after, she saw the red car backing down the drive. When she had finished the dishes she sat down in the living-room and closed her eyes. For some months she had been trying to tell herself that the tightness in her chest and the pain in her left arm when she did too much in the garden, particularly if the wind was cold, was just a muscle strain, but what was the point in trying to delude herself? She was quite familiar with the symptoms of angina. One of the troubles was that Roberta was so intolerant of illness in any shape or form – 'all in the mind' was one of her favourite expressions – and a cardiac invalid hanging about the house was the last thing she would want. That wasn't the whole of it, either, Roberta was utterly hopeless domestically and would be completely lost should anything happen to her.

Amelia Pelton was still sitting there some ten minutes later, lacking the energy to get on with the housework, when there was a short, sharp ring on the front door bell. She got up and looked out of the window, but it had started to rain and the person outside was not in view; no doubt, she thought, standing right up against the door under the porch.

It took her a few moments to undo the chain, Roberta having left by the back door. When she got it open all that she found was a shoe-box lying on the mat. It was secured by some tightly knotted string. She carried it back into the sitting-room, put it on Roberta's desk, slipped the plain brown envelope with her name typed on it from beneath the twine and slit it open with the paperknife. She scanned the photograph and the single sheet of paper, which had been inside it, then sat down heavily on the chair and read it again.

'Recognize this piece of china? It was found in Belling's summer-house where Linda Baines and your dear "friend" Roberta used to behave in a blatantly immoral fashion. You don't believe me? Take a look at the photograph, then. Quite artistic, isn't it? There were others, too, that are distinctly more anatomical. Did Roberta really just find Linda's body, or was she responsible for putting it in the wood? I wonder. Do you?'

Amelia Pelton didn't really need to remove the tissue paper to confirm what she suspected already, but she did so, taking out the delicate porcelain figure and lifting it up. She inspected the base in the vain hope of finding that it was a different one, but there, in front of her eyes, was the slight stain that had been present on the day she had bought it.

The photograph, too, had unquestionably been taken by

Roberta, in the studio in the loft – Amelia recognized the backcloth, which her friend had used before when doing her still-life studies. The picture of Linda had been taken in soft focus; the girl was standing naked with her back to the camera, looking at herself dreamily in the full-length mirror on its wooden stand. She had no difficulty in recognizing that either; she had, after all, seen it every day for the last forty- odd years standing in the corner of their bedroom.

The woman shook her head. There could be no denying that Linda had been a really lovely girl, but that only made it worse. Had Roberta stopped at photographing her? Even if she had, it didn't make it much better and she had obviously given the girl the Meissen figurine. Somehow, too, its having happened in the house they had shared for so long made it that much worse – Roberta must have taken advantage of the day she, Amelia, had gone up to London to see the exhibition of French impressionists at the National Gallery.

The studio was locked, as it always was, but this was no time for half-measures. Amelia Pelton went out to the garden shed, brought in the old coal hammer and, even though it was extremely difficult to keep her balance from half-way up the ladder, which they kept in the built-in cupboard on the landing, she managed to get in enough solid blows to deform and eventually break open the combination padlock. At the end of it, the sweat was standing out on her forehead and her heart was pounding in her chest. It was all she could do to push up the heavy trap-door and climb into the loft.

Roberta was a methodical person, the negatives were all filed according to date and it took Amelia only a few minutes to locate them. Even through the magnifying-glass from the darkroom, the fine detail was not clear, but even so it was perfectly obvious that Roberta had not failed to make the most of her opportunity. Every part of Linda's body had been scrutinized by the lens; there were full-length shots and close-ups taken at a variety of different angles, some in black-and-white and some in colour. While some of the poses were artistic, others were unspeakably crude.

Amelia Pelton put them back as she had found them and went back down the stairs, getting her own albums out and opening the earliest one. Roberta had been so handsome then in her WRNS uniform and just as full of life as she was now. Her energy hadn't even been all that much diminished when she was convalescing from her attack of typhoid. Roberta had gone up to Kashmir to escape the heat of Delhi and as she had some leave owed to her Amelia went with her. It was an idyllic time; they had got to know each other properly, their relationship developed and towards the end of their time there neither had any doubt that they were going to spend the rest of their lives together.

She flicked over the pages. Roberta on horseback, Roberta swimming and Roberta playing tennis – how it brought back the memories. She paused when she came to another picture, this time of Roberta on the rifle-range. Her friend was lying prone and squinting along the sights of an old army Lee Enfield. This time the memory was a much more disturbing one.

They had been in bed one night in their bungalow when Amelia, always a light sleeper, had woken up suddenly. For a moment, she was unable to place what had disturbed her, but then she heard the faint sound from the next room.

'Roberta,' she whispered urgently, 'Roberta, wake up!'

'What is it?'

'There's someone in the next room.'

Roberta hadn't hesitated. She slipped out of bed, her body white in the moonlight, and, taking her revolver out of the drawer in the bedside table, crept to the door.

'Do be careful,' Amelia said softly.

'Shut up,' Roberta mouthed, beckoning her friend to come across the room. 'Listen,' she whispered in her ear, 'when I drop my hand, open the door, turn on the light in the next room and then duck down quickly. Got it?'

Amelia did as she was told and let out a cry when she saw the oiled body clad in a loincloth only six feet from her. He raised his arm and she opened her eyes wide in horror as he took a step forward and the blade of the vicious-looking kukri began to descend. As she stood there transfixed, the shot rang out, there was a loud metallic clang and the weapon flew out of the robber's hand. For one moment he stared at the naked woman facing him, then began to gibber with terror as she advanced with the revolver pointed straight at him.

'Do you know what, little man, I'm going to teach you a lesson you'll not forget in a hurry.'

'Roberta, no!'

The second shot rang out as she let out the despairing cry. At the man's scream she ran across to the bed, throwing herself face down on it, her body racked with sobs.

'It's all right, old thing, I only winged the bugger. It's nothing much despite the noise he's making and you wouldn't have wanted me to let him run away and prey on defenceless women again, now would you?' She let out a short laugh and picked her dressing-gown up off the chair. 'Come on, hop into bed and I'll go and deal with that stupid prick.'

After that incident Amelia viewed Roberta with a respect bordering on awe, but tinged with fear and concern. Her friend had enjoyed the whole episode, she was sure of it, and over the following years the same streak of cruelty surfaced from time to time. Occasionally it had even been directed at her and if it had usually been purely verbal, that was by no means always the case.

Had Roberta killed Linda? The more Amelia thought about it, the more likely it seemed to be. It was obvious that the girl had not stolen the figurine and that she must have been given it; why else would Roberta have made up that story about Louis having knocked it off the table? She had been incredibly gullible to have believed her friend's explanation at the time; the ornament would hardly have been smashed to pieces by falling a mere couple of feet on to the carpet. Had Linda been black-mailing Roberta? That seemed probable, too, particularly as the girl had obviously managed to get hold of several of the prints from the negatives upstairs. Roberta's motive was strong enough; a major part of her life revolved around the village and the golf-club and she must have realized that once the fact of her having taken those pictures came out, she would be thrown out and people like Geoffrey Belling and Charles Crichton, men she admired and respected, would never speak to her again. And what would the hot-tempered George Baines do? Come looking for her with his shotgun in all probability. The two of them would have had to leave Welbury and that would have broken Roberta's heart.

Amelia had been lying when she had told the policeman that Roberta had been terribly upset at finding Linda's body. She hadn't, not in the least; it had been almost the same as that time in India when she had shot the robber. She had been on a high, unable to stop talking, recounting all the details over and over again. Afterwards she had, as on that previous occasion, been sexually demanding and aggressive.

She went through the rest of the albums, which charted the history of their relationship, the ups and the downs, the highs and the lows and then she let out a deep sigh. If Roberta had felt the need for someone like Linda, would she, even at her age, be looking for other diversions in the future, even to the extent of leaving her if her heart began to play up even more? And would she herself want to go on living with a woman whom she believed to be a murderess? And what was going to happen now that someone else clearly knew what had occurred?

She was feeling too upset even to start thinking about who that someone else might be, but the answers to the other questions left her in no doubt about what she had to do. She put the albums away, cleaned up the mess she had made on the landing and went into the kitchen. She put a match to the letter and washed the ash down the sink. Afterwards, she went up to the bathroom and swallowed all the sleeping-pills in the bottle in the medicine cabinet. Finally, she put the Meissen shepherd girl with the picture of Linda propped against it on the dressing-table where she could see them both, took off her shoes and lay down on the bed …

'Pelton, I'm back. Where are you? Pelton, are you all right?'

The voice seemed to be coming from a very long way away and although she struggled to open her eyes, the effort was too much for her.

'Pelton! My God, what have you done?'

Somehow, it made it a great deal worse to be aware of what was going on and yet not be able to do anything about it. She was wrapped in a blanket, carried carefully down to the car and then had to suffer the pain and indignity of the plastic tubing being forced down her throat at the cottage hospital. Most humiliating of all was the realization, when she had been tucked up in the side room off the female ward, that she hadn't even been able to make a proper job of killing herself.

Roberta Pargeter put the car into first gear, pressed the accelerator until the needle of the rev counter was hovering near the red segment on the dial and then slid her foot sideways off the clutch. Back wheels spinning and the rear end snaking under the fierce acceleration, the red car shot past the hospital, up the hill and out of the village. Only after she had driven some ten miles and come within an ace of a head-on collision with a tractor which was trundling around a corner, in the centre of the road, did she slow down and turn back towards Welbury.

In place of her previous uncontrolled rage there was now cold anger at what had happened. She was going to find out who had driven Amelia to attempted suicide and then God help him or her! On arriving at the house she went upstairs. Seeing the broken padlock she understood at once that it was worse than she had realized. All the negatives were there, but she had always been punctilious about handling them only by their edges and now there were clear finger-marks on all the ones of Linda. She collected them all together in their neat packets, gathered up several others from her collection as well and, before doing anything else, took them down to her safe-deposit box at the bank.

Back at the house, she put the shepherdess on the table in the living-room, placing the photograph of Linda against it, and sat in one of the armchairs looking at it. Why had she been such a fool? The simple answer was that, even at her age, she hadn't been able to help herself. She had joked to the detective about Cyril Atherton's reaction to the girl's streak, but she had been just as affected herself; the sight of Linda's naked body had hit her with a force that was physical in its intensity – there had been a tight, painful constriction in her chest and she hadn't been able to get her breath properly for several minutes. There was no choice in the matter; she just had to see the girl again and, although it took the exercise of some ingenuity, she achieved it quite quickly. She got Amelia to agree to having some help in the garden and then had a chat to Geoffrey Belling about it at the club. It wasn't long before the girl's name came up and she was willing to bet that, if asked, the man would have sworn that it had been his idea.

'You're very beautiful, you know, Linda,' she said one day, when Amelia was at the church and the girl was having a coffee-break with her in the sitting-room. 'Have you ever thought of doing any modelling?'

'Yes, I have, but I'm not tall enough. I asked Miss Pembleton about it.'

'Models don't only work with clothes, you know.'

'How do you mean?'

'There are figure studies as well.'

'You're talking about page three girls?'

'That sort of thing.'

Linda was sharp enough; she had known straight away what she was getting at, even before she asked her directly; Roberta could see that from the expression on her face, which was one of excitement and, more than that, one of calculation as well.

'Would you pose for me? I have a studio here in the loft.'

'I might. It depends.'

'On what?'

'What you want me to do and what it's going to be worth.'

'I'll give you a hundred if you strip off completely.'

'Make it two and give me that china ornament and I'll do the lot.'

'The lot?'

'Anything you like.'

Roberta explained to the girl that the figurine was one of a pair and that they were of special sentimental value to her, but Linda was adamant – no china ornament, no posing. Roberta eventually gave in and the girl's little smile of triumph said it all – she knew the power she had all right. She kept her side of the bargain, though. When Amelia was in London, Linda spent two hours in the studio and although she refused any physical contact, hinting that that might be open to negotiation later on if the terms were right, she did allow herself to be photographed in whatever way was requested and totally without inhibition.

It was not long after that that Roberta decided that it would be too risky to allow Linda to continue to work for Amelia. The girl was getting cheeky and, as for herself, she was finding it increasingly difficult to keep her hands off her. And so she dismissed her, with suitable compensation, of course, on the grounds that Amelia was getting suspicious, which in fact, she realized, might not have been far from the truth. The other worry was that Linda had been getting too demanding for comfort; she wanted some photographs of herself, saying that they might help her to get a modelling job and hinted that there might be problems for Roberta if her request was not granted. She did give the girl three of the most innocuous prints, but enough was enough and there and then she decided it would have to stop.

Roberta gave a deep sigh and went through into the kitchen to make herself a cup of tea. It was when she was filling the kettle that she noticed the small piece of charred paper and traces of ash in the sink.

'Pull yourself together, Pargeter,' she said to herself, 'and think.'

The ash must have come from a note – it certainly wasn't the remains of photographic paper in the sink – and the porcelain figure would hardly have been left without any wrapping, let alone handed to Amelia at the door. Her friend was a creature of habit; she always used the paper-knife for opening letters and scissors for cutting string and it shouldn't be too difficult to find some evidence, unless, of course, she had burned the lot. The shoe-box, which most certainly hadn't been there before, was in almost the first place she looked: the waste-paper basket by her desk. There was a label on it showing that it had originally contained trainers and from that and their size, it surely must have belonged to Linda originally. But who had brought it round and where had it been found?

Roberta had always found that making notes was an aid to thought, so she sat at the desk, pulled a piece of rough paper towards her and wrote: *where was it found?* on the left hand side and *by whom?* on the right. The two questions were obviously connected. If Linda had kept the figurine in her bedroom at the lodge, then either her father or Geoffrey Belling would have been the most likely ones to have discovered it, or perhaps even the police. She rejected Baines straight away. The man could not possibly have known that she was the owner of the figurine and certainly wouldn't have connected the photograph with it. Writing notes to Amelia wouldn't have been his style, either; he would have come charging round intent on violent retribution.

Belling? He certainly knew about and had admired the Meissen figures, was a keen photographer himself and was well aware of her own interest and expertise, but surely he, of all people, wouldn't have behaved like that. Sinclair was clearly no fool, he was trained to notice things and must also have seen the remaining shepherd-boy on the mantelpiece, drawing the obvious conclusion if he had come across the other one, but he would certainly have confronted her with the evidence directly.

There were two other more likely suspects, Helen Crichton and Cyril Atherton. Neither of them liked her, they both not only disapproved of her relationship with Amelia, but would have been quite capable of behaving in a vindictive and underhand way as well. If it had been either of them, though, how the hell had they got hold of the objects? Would Amelia be prepared to tell her what was in the note? She somehow doubted it. If only her friend hadn't burned it.

She had just written down the two further names on the sheet of paper and was fiddling with her pen when she saw the brown envelope, which was lying upside down near the paper-knife. It had to be the one. The photograph fitted inside it and 'Miss Amelia Pelton' was typed on the outside. The instrument was clearly an old one and hadn't she read somewhere that individual typewriters were as identifiable as fingerprints? Ever since she had seen

Amelia lying semi-conscious on the bed she had been determined to find the person responsible, and now, surely, she had the means at her disposal, even if it meant hiring a private detective.

Amelia didn't refuse to see her the following afternoon, which was the earliest she was allowed to visit, but she might just as well have done so. Her friend wouldn't say a word to her, resolutely turning her back and although Roberta admitted to having taken the photographs of Linda and giving her the shepherd-girl, she reassured her that there had been nothing more to it than that. She said several times how desperately sorry she was and that it wouldn't happen again. That produced no reaction either.

After she had been to the visitors' lavatory on the ground floor she decided to go back to have one more try. She had just gone through the main door to the ward when she caught sight of Inspector Sinclair in the cubicle. He was saying something to Amelia with great emphasis and she was not only listening, but looking at him as well. Immediately, Roberta shrank back and hurried down the stairs to wait in her car. What was the man doing there and how had he heard so quickly about Amelia's suicide attempt? Surely Dr Crichton wouldn't have told him – the man was an absolute stickler for medical etiquette.

For one moment, when she followed the detective and he turned into the main street, she thought he was going to her house, but he stopped short near the church, got out of his car without looking round and walked through the graveyard to the west door. He disappeared inside and, cursing the fact that her car was so conspicuous, she drove straight past, put it in her garage and hurried back. There was a screen of trees running along the side of the graveyard and she was able to keep watch without any risk of detection. She didn't have long to wait. Some five minutes later Sinclair reappeared, hesitated for a moment in the porch, took a careful look round, then walked quickly back to his car and drove off, this time taking the opposite direction out of the village towards the Oxford road.

What was all that about, she wondered? Surely, if the detective had come to see Atherton, he would have stayed longer and if the man wasn't there, why hadn't he come out sooner and then tried the vicarage, which was a mere hundred yards away? Had Amelia been suspicious of the man and was that why Sinclair had gone round to see him? When she went inside, the church was empty, as was the vestry. As she left she glanced idly at the notice-board just inside the porch.

'Good God!' she said out loud.

Amongst various leaflets and notices of services, there was an announcement typewritten on headed notepaper, which merely read:

'The choir practice on Thursday next has been cancelled owing to the illness of Miss Searby. It is hoped to hold one next week as usual.'

The type as a whole was of poor quality, but it was the same instrument as the one used for the envelope addressed to Amelia – she was certain of it. The 'e's were out of alignment and the closed part of those letters was filled in. It was too much to hope that the typewriter was in the vestry, but none the less she went back to have a look before returning home.

It just had to be Atherton, but why had the man been so careless? Perhaps he didn't care if he was found out, or perhaps, more likely, he was just an unpractised criminal. There was the third possibility that someone else had used his typewriter, but she didn't believe that. If it had been the vicar, then he would still have the other two prints of Linda and of course he would want to keep them; hadn't his eyes been out on stalks when she had done her streak?

Roberta found her old service-revolver in the cabin-trunk in the attic, in the part adjacent to her studio, where it had been since 1947, when she had returned from the East. The barrel was rusty and she wouldn't have trusted it to stay in one piece or the two remaining bullets to go off if she had tried to fire it, but Atherton wouldn't know that and at least it was still possible to cock it impressively.

She waited until 10.30 and then walked the 200 yards to the vicarage. There was a light on in one of the downstairs windows. Through the window she saw the man sitting at his roll-top desk, studying something with a magnifying-glass. If all else failed, she thought, she could always ring the bell, but the front door was within sight of the road and if Atherton created a major fuss it would be bound to attract someone's attention, so she walked round to the rear of the house. No wonder, she thought a minute or two later, that Bert Stringer had been so scathing about house-hold security in his talk to the Neighbourhood Watch group; the back door was unlocked and she walked straight into the kitchen and out into the hall.

She was standing there, undecided what to do next, when she heard Atherton's cough and the creak of a floor-board. Without thinking she stepped through the door immediately to her right, pulling it to behind her. Was it cowardice or prudence that prevented her from confronting him there and then? When she considered the matter later she liked to think that it was the latter, but whatever the reason she stayed in what was obviously the dining-room until he had stopped moving about downstairs and she heard the bath being filled on the floor above and the antiquated plumbing gurgling and clanking.

She went out into the hall and through the door of the study. She had just shut it behind her when the water stopped running and she heard Atherton clear his throat as he descended the stairs. Pulling the revolver out of the waistband of her trousers, she stepped back, her heart thumping wildly, but he must, she thought, merely have forgotten something in the kitchen, for a few minutes later she heard him going back up to the first floor. Quickly pulling the curtains to and blocking the gap under the door with a rug, she switched on the light and went straight to the desk.

The only drawer that was locked was the top right-hand one. After looking through the others and typing a few words on a sheet of paper with the ancient machine she pulled the drawer immediately below the locked one right out and felt above with her hand. As she had hoped, not only was the drawer not in a separate partition, but the wood of its base was both thin and split throughout its length. When she inserted the blade of the steel paper-knife and pushed it upwards and sideways, the gap widened sufficiently to allow her to get her gloved fingers into it. After a series of sharp tugs the wood splintered and she was able to extract the contents of the drawer. Roberta smiled when she saw the girlie magazine; she had always known that the man was a sanctimonious hypocrite and here was the proof of it. That wasn't all; the two photographs of Linda were hidden between its pages. No wonder he had been peering so intently through his magnifying-glass.

After that slice of luck she decided not to chance her arm any further. When she had replaced the drawer, switched off the light, opened the curtains and put back the rug, she paused at the door, listening. She had not heard the bath-water running out and now seemed as good a time as any to leave. She had only just had time to open the door an inch or two when the burglar alarm went off in the hall. For one moment she was paralysed into inactivity by the appalling noise, then she ran out into the kitchen, breathed a sigh of relief when she saw that the key was still in the back door and ran down the side of the house behind the trees. She was just slipping in through her garden gate, when the voice came from directly behind her.

'What's that infernal din about?'

She whirled round to see Alan Marple, her neighbour.

'Sounds like a burglar alarm. I came out to investigate, but couldn't see anything.'

'Bloody awful things – always going off accidentally. Good-night.'

'Good-night.'

She was getting too old for this sort of thing, Roberta thought as she settled Louis down for the night, feeling her pulse still racing. Perhaps it was just as well that she hadn't met Atherton face to face – there was no knowing what people might do when cornered. Anyway, it looked as if Sinclair was interested in him and that should take care of things satisfactorily. From now on, she thought, a distinctly low profile was indicated, the lower the better.

CHAPTER TEN

Fiona had a battle with her conscience over the question of whether or not it would be fair to leave seeing Helen Crichton until the Tuesday morning and eventually settled for a compromise by ringing her up on the Monday morning.

'May I come to see you tomorrow at about nine?' she asked when she had got through. 'I should have something to tell you by then.'

'Be my guest, I've got nothing else to do, but why so bloody early?'

'I've got to be back in Oxford by twelve. How are you feeling?'

'Still on the wagon, if that's what you were worried about.'

'That's good news.'

'You can cut out the sarcasm.'

'I'll see you tomorrow, then.'

When she had rung off Fiona saw herself in the mirror in the hall. The sight of her frown and her lips clamped together was just what was needed to break the tension. To hell with Helen Crichton, she thought; there was no need to think about the bloody woman for a full twenty-four hours. Was it really less than a week since she had started to work with Sinclair? It felt like a lifetime.

Trying to get her mind off the case, she gave her flat a good clean and then went for a long walk along the river before coming back for a leisurely bath and a hair-wash. Even that didn't work, though; there had been something niggling away at the back of her mind and that was Helen Crichton's manner on the telephone. She knew that she wouldn't have any peace of mind until she had made quite sure that the woman was all right. After the evening rush hour was over she drove to London. Even if she was wrong, she thought, it would save her a trip the following day.

On her way there, she tried to marshal her thoughts about the case. It had never made sense to her that Helen Crichton should have knocked Linda off her bike, battered her to death with a stone and arranged things to make it look as if she had been raped. If she had been under the influence of alcohol, she surely would never have even thought about doing anything so complicated and … Anyway, she thought, now that the woman had an alibi, there was no point in considering her further. The simu-lated rape still worried her – it seemed such an extraordinary thing to set up. Perhaps the man about to do it had been interrupted by something. It could hardly have been Miss Pargeter – Rawlings seemed quite confident that the girl had been dead for some time before she had been found. What about her other idea? That didn't fit in with what Rawlings had found, either, and the pathologist had the reputation of being infallible.

When Helen Crichton answered the door, Fiona was shocked to see the state that the woman was in. Not only was there no trace of her previous aggression, but the self-possession she had seemed to be showing when she had last seen her had evaporated and a muscle was twitching under her left eye.

'What's up? Has anything else happened? You look awful.'

'It's just that I'm so scared. Someone's going to kill me, I just know they are. They'll find out that I'm here and … I just don't know what to do and I can't take it much longer.'

'You'll be all right. Your husband is the only person in the village who knows where you are and I'm sure he won't have told anyone else.'

'You don't know Charles. He likes talking to people and then there was that phone call.'

'What phone call?'

'Some man asking for Charles's brother, Paul.'

'Why should that bother you'? Did he say anything else?'

'Just that he was sorry to have bothered me when I told him that Paul was in America, but there was something about his voice; it was a bit rough and I was almost sure that I'd heard it before.'

'I expect it was just your imagination playing tricks.' The woman shook her head and began to cry softly. 'Don't worry, you'll be quite safe here.'

'I'm so scared. You wouldn't stay here for the night, would you? I promise I'll find somewhere else to go tomorrow.'

It was the very last thing Fiona wanted to do, but suppose the wretched woman were to take an overdose of the sleeping pills that she had found in the medicine cabinet or cut her wrists? She knew perfectly well that she wouldn't be able to live with herself were that to happen. She found some pyjamas belonging to Paul Crichton in the chest of drawers and with Helen seeming a lot calmer now that she had agreed to stay, got into bed.

Fiona slept very badly and when she heard the clock from the local church strike seven, she decided to have another five minutes in bed before getting up. She came to with a start and saw to her dismay that it was nearly nine. If she didn't get a move on, she would be late for her appointment with Sinclair. She went into the bathroom, had a quick wash, ran a comb through her hair and, as she came out, heard the clink of crockery coming from the kitchen.

Fiona couldn't help wondering what sort of constitution the woman must have; gone was the self-pitying tearfulness of the previous evening and she even made quite a good breakfast.

'Look, I'm sorry about the way I've been behaving, I really am,' Helen said, when they were drinking their coffee. 'I've been an absolute shit. Everything was happening at once, I was fool enough to take another drink yesterday afternoon, I began to feel sorry for myself and ...'

'That's all right, I've been pretty rude myself.'

'No more than I deserved.'

'Well, you were right about your friend Earnshaw.'

'So he denied the whole thing, I suppose.'

'Yes, he did, but not to worry, I was able to get confirmation of what you told Inspector Sinclair.'

'And how did you achieve that miracle?'

'There were a couple of small boys in the loft that Sunday afternoon.'

'And they saw the lot?' Fiona nodded. 'God! Not the nun bit?'

'Yes and not only that; they had been there earlier and watched the nurse and gorilla bits as well.'

'The little bastards!'

The woman bent over the table and buried her face in

her hands, her shoulders shaking. Fiona was on the point of getting up to comfort her when she realized that Helen Crichton wasn't crying, she was laughing, laughing so much that she was almost completely out of control.

'My God!' she said, when she had recovered, 'that did me good, I can hardly remember the last time I had a really good laugh, one that was genuine and unforced. I was just thinking what Alec must have looked like from up in that loft, let alone me. I can't see him seeing it in that light, though; Alec never did have a sense of humour.' The woman wiped her streaming eyes. 'Do you know something? I like you. You're just about the only person in the last few years who's been direct with me and who's done what they say they're going to do and it makes a refreshing change, I can tell you. Do you have any idea who was responsible for killing Linda Baines?'

'Not at the moment, but we do have one or two leads that we are in the process of following up. I'll let you know how it turns out.'

'Thanks. You know, you may not believe it after what I did yesterday, but I've been thinking about a job and it might just be the answer I've been looking for, once the dust's settled. If Charles doesn't like it, he can lump it and who knows, he may even like it, particularly if it keeps me off the drink.'

'Do you seriously think you'll be able to achieve that?'

'What? Keep off the drink? Do you know, I think I can. It may sound far-fetched, but I've not really wanted to until this morning. Why the sudden conversion? I think it's the realization that someone actually cares about what happened to me and I never dreamt that that someone might be a policewoman. I know that sounds sloppy and facile, but it happens to be true.'

'It's nice of you to say so, but I could cheerfully have strangled you last night!'

'I wouldn't have blamed you if you had.'

'What I can't understand is how you manage to pick up so quickly afterwards. I hardly drink at all, but if I overdo it, I feel absolutely terrible the next day, whereas you seem to be able to shrug it off with no trouble at all.'

'It's partly the luck of having the right constitution, I suppose, but I'll also let you into a secret; I don't drink anything like as much as my reputation in Welbury would have you believe. If people think you're drunk the whole time, it gives you a licence to behave badly and say outrageous things. It's only when I'm really unhappy or under stress that I well and truly hit the bottle – it's a psychological rather than a physical dependence. Don't get me wrong, I know that a lot of drinkers say the same thing and that I've been playing with fire, but in my case it happens to be true. I'm deeply ashamed to have to admit it, but although I was flat out when you and your boss found me here, I wasn't yesterday. What I said and did was just play-acting and designed to wind you up. It was when I saw you looking so tired and fed up this morning that, as I said before, I realized what an utter shit I'd been. I really meant it when I said I was sorry.'

They chatted for another quarter of an hour, then, after promising to give her a ring that evening, Fiona got up to go.

Helen Crichton showed her to the door. When she opened it she looked out and up at the sky.

'You'd better take Paul's umbrella; it looks as if the heavens are about to open.'

'It's all right, my car's only on the other side of the road.'

'Go on. There's another one here and you can bring it back when it's convenient.'

'All right. Thanks.'

Fiona unfurled the golfing umbrella in the area and started up the steps. It was rather a tight fit at the top and when she couldn't hear any drops falling on it she tilted it sideways, looking up when she reached street-level. Everything happened with terrifying speed; she had the impression of something moving above her, there was a sudden brilliant flash of lightning, a loud sizzling sound, the smell of ozone and almost simultaneously a tremendous crash of thunder. For a second she stood rooted to the spot, then took an involuntary pace backwards. She just had time to register that she had missed the step before something hit the umbrella and she fell, tumbling down into the basement area.

The press conference was an empty charade. Everyone there knew that Watson wasn't going to give away any hard information and yet they went through the usual pantomime of predictable questions. Are you expecting an early breakthrough? Do you think a local man was responsible for the crime? Will the killer strike again?

Bill Watson's performance was predictable, but none the less impressive for that. He looked and sounded exactly what he was, dogged, dependable and honest. No, an arrest wasn't imminent; yes, they had some promising lines of inquiry, no, he couldn't give any details just yet; yes, he would do so at the earliest possible opportunity.

Part of the journalists' frustration no doubt stemmed from the fact that once they had filmed the police searching the wood there was nothing else for them to put on camera. They had tried to interview Miss Pargeter and been told precisely what they could do with themselves for their pains, and Belling had effectively put a stop to anyone getting anywhere near either Baines or Tracey Farrell. The best they had been able to achieve was a brief interview with the headmaster of Linda's school, who merely said how popular and what a promising athlete the girl had been and how shocked everyone was.

Sinclair sat on Watson's left both at the press conference and for the short filmed interview for TV, but didn't have to say a word, doing his best to follow Watson's instructions, which were to look alert and confident and keep his mouth shut.

After it was all over Watson had a word with him in his office.

'I've been thinking about what you told me yesterday and I'm very pleased with the progress you've made so far. Need any more help?'

'Not just for the moment, thank you, sir.'

'What do you plan to do next?'

'Keep up the pressure on Belling, Atherton, Mrs Crichton and Miss Pargeter and interview Dr Crichton, whom I haven't had time to see yet.'

'Any thoughts about dressing up that DC of yours in the right clothes and getting her to cycle on the route Linda Baines probably took?'

'I doubt if it would help.'

'Quite possibly not, but the press like that sort of thing. By the way, how is she shaping up?'

'Fiona Campbell?'

'Yes.'

'Extremely well. She's quick on the uptake, knows when and how much initiative to take and has a happy knack of being able to get people to talk.'

'Good. Glad to hear it.'

Sinclair went back to his office and while waiting for Fiona, began to write down the names of possible suspects. The one thing – which he had told Watson on the previous day – that made it certain that the murderer was a local man, and he was quite sure that it was a man, was that he had been too clever by half. If he hadn't tried to incriminate Helen Crichton, anyone could have been responsible, although Rawlings's view that the girl hadn't been raped certainly took a bit of explaining.

And what about the various suspects? The forensic people had come up with the fact that the cigarette-ends came from Benson & Hedges Special Filter, a brand that both Atherton and Belling smoked, but different from the one that Fiona had taken from the summer-house. If Belling had dropped them it was just possible that there was an innocent explanation, but that didn't apply to the trampled-down undergrowth. Was Linda blackmailing him? Was he the one who had been providing her with money and more presents than he had admitted to? After his early return from Birmingham, did he take a walk round his garden, hear what Linda was up to – according to Tracey Farrell she had been making a good deal of noise – and then did he follow her and kill her in a fit of jealousy? Belling didn't seem to be the type to kill anyone, but Sinclair had to admit that he had been wrong about people before. He made a mental note to take a look at the man's Jaguar; the scene-of-crime men seemed quite sure that the pedal on Linda's bicycle had been hit by a car.

Then there was Atherton. He was also a smoker and he clearly believed that the girl was possessed by the devil in a very literal sense. According to Miss Pargeter, he was guilt-ridden over sex. Had it all boiled over that afternoon? Sinclair had believed from the beginning that Linda's murderer was a male, but was he right to eliminate the mannish Roberta Pargeter? It was true that she had joked about the streak, but she had clearly been affected by Linda, too, and it looked as if she had given, or had been forced to give, the girl the figurine. Had Linda allowed her sexual favours in return for that and financial inducements as well? The woman had found the body, she was undoubtedly a very tough nut and she and Helen Crichton were clearly at daggers drawn. It wouldn't have taken her long to go back to the Crichtons' house, break the trafficator cover and put the pieces on the road. Had she made it look like rape to suggest that a man was responsible?

Could Charles Crichton be ruled out? According to Fiona he had seemed quite straightforward when talking about Linda, and his wife had withdrawn her allegations about him feeling the girl up. Finally, there seemed little doubt that he had done an excellent job in looking after Rose Baines and supporting George. He was, though, the one suspect whom he hadn't seen. He clearly needed to remedy the deficiency before very long. And what about Baines himself? Hadn't he read somewhere that the stress of incest could lead to behaviour such as Linda's? Suppose the man had gone to look for his daughter, found her and ...

Sinclair's thoughts were interrupted by the telephone ringing.

'Yes, speaking.' He listened in silence for a few moments, then asked a series of crisp questions, nodding to himself when he heard the answers. 'Are you absolutely certain? ... Put Helen Crichton on the line, would you, please? ... Yes, of course I trust you; all I want to do is satisfy myself that she's in a fit state to guard you properly ... Just get her, would you? That's an order.' Helen came on the line a minute or two later.

'I'll be with you in about an hour and a half,' he went on, 'and listen, if there's any doubt in your mind, any doubt at all, you're to send for an ambulance. Is that quite clear? … Good.'

Dick Appleyard had been with him on the course at Hendon and Sinclair thanked his lucky stars that not only had the man been in his office at Scotland Yard when he rang, but that someone who was both on his wavelength and quick on the uptake should have been available. They had shared an interest in chess and had kept up their rivalry at first by telephone and then e-mail.

'I took you at your word,' Appleyard said as they drove out of Paddington Station, 'and I have left the basement flat alone, but a couple of my men have been up on the roof and should be through by now.'

'Thanks, I'm most grateful. Did you get an eye-witness account of what happened?'

'According to a man from one of the flats opposite, there was a flash of lightning, the crash of thunder and then the chimney came down, partly on to the pavement and partly into the basement area.'

'Anyone hurt on the street?'

'Just a woman walking by. Luckily nothing too serious, just a broken collar-bone and a cut on her scalp. The ambulance had already taken her to Mary's by the time I arrived.'

As they came round the corner Sinclair saw that traffic cones had been put around the rubble and a uniformed constable was standing on the steps leading to the main entrance to the building.

'When you've finished in the flat I'll either be out here or up on the roof,' Appleyard said when the car came to a halt.

'OK, thanks.'

Sinclair picked his way carefully down the steps leading to the basement flat. He paused at the bottom. The bulk of the chimney had hit the pavement, but even so there was a substantial amount of rubble down here and it was obvious that Fiona had had a very lucky escape indeed. Helen Crichton opened the door almost at once in response to his knock. To his relief she looked a different person from the one he had seen before. She appeared alert and had even put on some make-up.

'How is she?'

'Quite badly bruised and with some nasty grazes, but otherwise she's fine.'

Fiona was lying on the divan in the bedroom. She made no attempt to get up when he went in; she was pale and drawn with a nasty abrasion on the side of her face which was weeping and angry-looking, but she was still able to manage a smile.

'Well now, what have you been up to?'

He sat down on the side of the bed while she explained that she had decided to visit Helen the previous day and why she had stayed the night.

'And you think that the chimney was deliberately pushed down on you?'

'Yes. I'm absolutely certain that it started to move before I saw the lightning and even though the flash was very close, it certainly didn't hit the roof above me. I think it must have been my instinctive jump backwards that saved me, even though that meant that I fell down the steps, which caused most of the damage. I'm pretty sure that I was only hit by a small piece of the masonry.'

'And you also think that it was meant for Helen Crichton?'

'It must have been. Whoever was up on the roof could only have seen the umbrella, not that I was under it, and Helen did go out with it yesterday, when the same person must have been watching.'

'But presumably they didn't realize that you were in the flat as well.'

'I imagine not. Helen is also quite sure that it was meant for her, which is one of the reasons why we decided between us to stay put until you came. She was terrified of being left alone and of the person responsible having another go if she went outside to an ambulance with me.'

'But what about you? I suppose it's too much to expect her to have given you a thought.'

'No, that's not fair – she was amazing. She got me back in here out of the rain and she really knew what to do, having worked for a year in accident and emergency at St Mary's some years ago. She checked to make sure that nothing was broken, then helped me under the shower and got all the dust and muck out of my hair, before putting a dressing on the graze on my back. She helped me over the shock, too – we had a long chat while we were waiting for you. She's really nice once one gets to know her a bit.'

'Well, I hope she's duly grateful to you as well.'

'All this might be just the jolt she's been needing.'

Pigs might fly, Sinclair thought; he knew about alcoholics, but this was clearly not the time to upset Fiona by expressing his disbelief at Helen Crichton's miraculous conversion to sobriety and he managed to smile reassuringly.

'I certainly hope so. Now, all right if I go up the steps and see if they've found anything?'

'They?'

Sinclair explained what he had arranged with Inspector Appleyard. Before leaving he said to her, with mock severity:

'After that, Fiona, it's off to hospital with you.'

'Do I have to go?'

'You certainly do.'

'But my anti-tetanus injections are up to date.'

'You'll need a proper check and if the graze on your back is anything like as bad as the one on your face, you'll need to have that cleaned and dressed properly. All right?'

'I suppose so. I won't have to stay there, will I?'

'We'll have to see.'

'What about Helen?'

'I'll have to think about her, too. If you're right about what happened, she most certainly ought not to stay here and I can't see her being prepared to go back to Welbury.' He got up from the bed. 'Right, I won't be very long.'

The constable was still standing outside on the pavement when Sinclair went up the steps.

'Inspector Appleyard's on the roof, sir, and said to meet him up there. There's a way up at the top of the staircase.'

Sinclair nodded to the man, walked up the four flights of stairs inside the house and then climbed the telescopic ladder, which was resting against the surround of the open skylight.

'How's it going, Dick?'

'Your woman was quite right,' the man replied, straightening up. 'Despite the downpour, there's clear evidence that someone's been up on the roof here recently. He probably came over the neighbouring ones – this skylight obviously hadn't been opened for years.'

'How about the chimney-stack?'

Appleyard pointed to his right. 'You can see that the

mortar around what's left of the base is in very poor condition, but there are some fresh chisel-marks on the brick and even though the surrounding area has been cleaned up pretty thoroughly, our man found some flakes of brick.'

He held up the plastic bag for Sinclair to see.

'So you think someone did push it down?'

The man nodded. 'I'm as near certain as I can be at this stage and there's no sign of a lightning-strike. It wouldn't have taken much effort, either; that other stack over there is extremely rocky – try it for yourself.'

Sinclair went over to it and felt a distinct give as he leaned against it.

'Probably hasn't had any maintenance since it was built. No sign of anyone suspicious in the vicinity?'

Appleyard shook his head. 'One of our men's been along the top of the roofs in both directions and had a good look round with binoculars.'

Sinclair nodded. 'I'm just going to arrange for Fiona to have a check at St Mary's and then I wonder if you'd mind if I had a word with that old trot on the ground floor. She was sitting at her window when we arrived and she was still there when I came up here – she may well have seen something.'

'Good idea. I'll join you.'

CHAPTER ELEVEN

It had been the most exciting day that Ethel Cummings could remember, not least because of the visit from the two police-officers. The nice-looking one, too, proved to be absolutely charming, making friends with her cat, Mr Gladstone, accepting a cup of tea – she had been most careful not to offer either of them sherry as she knew that policemen never drank alcohol on duty – and congratulating her on her powers of observation.

'You don't mean to tell me that it wasn't the lightning that brought that chimney down?'

'Yes, I'm afraid that it looks very much as if it was pushed over and I think it quite possible that a man might have been watching this building in the last few days. Have you seen anything out of the ordinary during that time?'

The woman thought carefully before replying. 'Well,' she said eventually, 'there was one unusual thing. There are a lot of men around here during the afternoons and evenings; you see, there are two girls doing business in a couple of the basement flats across the road, if you get my meaning.'

'I get your meaning.'

'It's quite interesting in its way; some of their clients

walk in with confidence, some look around and then slip down the steps when they think that no one is looking and some, poor dears, give up and go away. Hardly any of them look very happy when they come out, either. Rather sad, isn't it?'

'Yes, it is.'

'Where was I? Oh yes, I was coming up the road yesterday morning with my shopping-bag and I saw a very smart new car on the other side of the road; it was black, but absolutely gleaming. The people around here can't afford cars like that, it was too early in the day for one of the girls' customers and you could have knocked me down with a feather when a smartly dressed chauffeur got out and helped me up the steps with my basket. I was rather nervous about it – one reads so many stories about men robbing old things like me by gaining access to their flats and houses – but I had no cause for alarm, he was absolutely charming.'

'What exactly did he do?'

'He was terribly strong; he lifted up my basket on wheels, which was full of shopping and extremely heavy, with one hand, held open the door for me and then saw me through my own front door.'

'Did you see him leave in the car?'

'Yes, I did.'

'Did he pick up a passenger?'

'No. Perhaps he was delivering something. You see, after I had put my shopping away and was looking out of the window, I saw him cross the road from this side and get in the car.'

'Did he drive off straight away?'

'Now you mention it, no, he didn't. He was there for quite some time, all of fifteen minutes, I would say.'

'Do you think he might have stayed in this building after he had carried your basket in?'

'You don't mean …? Surely not that nice man.'

'It's a possibility.'

'You surprise and shake me. I couldn't honestly say.'

'But you didn't see him out of the door after he had helped you.'

'No, I didn't.'

'How long do you reckon it took you to put away your shopping, before you looked out of the window to see him cross the road?'

'About ten minutes, I'd say.'

'What did the man look like?'

'He was quite short – I don't think he would have come up above your chin – and thick-set. He had on a grey suit and matching peaked cap and brown shoes. Oh yes, his shoes.'

'What about them?'

'One doesn't often see brightly polished shoes these days, more's the pity, but his were wonderful, quite wonderful – they really shone.'

'What about his hair?'

'I couldn't see much of it because of his cap, but it was very neat at the back and sides. I don't like long hair in men, do you, Inspector?'

'No, I don't.'

'I didn't think you would. As for earrings!'

'Would you recognize him again?'

'Most certainly if he spoke and wore that uniform. Will I have to pick him out in an identification parade?'

'I hope that won't be necessary. I'm most grateful to you for all your help, Miss Cummings.'

'It was a pleasure.'

*

When Sinclair arrived at St Mary's he found Helen Crichton in the casualty department, still waiting for Fiona to come out.

'Thank you for coming with Fiona and coping with everything so well; you did an excellent job and I'm most grateful.'

'It's nice of you to say so. It was about time I did something useful for a change. That chimney was meant for me, wasn't it?' Sinclair nodded. 'And I suppose it was the umbrella that caused the mistake, if you can put it that way.'

'I imagine so. You clearly mustn't return to that flat, or Welbury, for that matter. Anywhere else you can go?'

'My father's in New York at the moment – I suppose I could stay in his flat in Eaton Square. He has a resident couple who look after him and they do know me.'

'That sounds very satisfactory. Would you let me have the address and telephone number in case I need to contact you? I'll be going back to Maida Vale soon to pick up Fiona's car, so I'll be able to give you a lift if you need to collect any of your belongings. I'd rather you didn't go on your own; I don't think you're in any further danger there now, but better safe than sorry.'

'Thank you. May I wait until Fiona comes out? I'd like to find out how she is.'

'Of course.'

'I find it very difficult to know how to put this, Inspector, but I'm very grateful to you both, particularly Fiona. We had a long chat while we were waiting for you in the flat and it made me look at things in a very different way.'

She stopped abruptly as a nurse opened the swing-door at the side of the waiting-room and started to manoeuvre the wheelchair through it.

Sinclair got up from his chair and went across the room to help.

'What's the verdict?'

'As Helen thought,' Fiona said. 'Nothing broken, I'm glad to say, just a lot of bruises and the two grazes. They've been picking bits of brick out of me, which I could have done without.'

'That I can believe. What's all that?'

Fiona raised the paper bag she was carrying a fraction. 'Dressings for the graze on my back and some pain-killers.'

'They're not going to let you go, are they?'

'They certainly are – I told you I was all right.'

'I don't trust you an inch,' Sinclair said, his smile softening his words. 'I'm going to have a word with the doctor.'

He came back soon after and took her on one side.

'Well, he confirmed that you could leave, all right, but there's going to be no more work for you for a week or two and you're certainly not going to go back to your flat on your own.'

'I don't see why not.'

'Couldn't you go to your aunt in Reading for a bit?'

'She's got her hands full since my uncle had a stroke and she's not all that well herself.'

'I see. And what are you going to do about clothes? I can hardly drive you to Oxford wearing male pyjamas and a dressing-gown and your other things are only suitable for an incinerator. Why not stay here for the night and I'll bring you some stuff tomorrow morning?'

'Couldn't Helen buy me some basics at the local shops?'

'And what do you suppose she's going to do for money?'

'One of the things she was able to salvage was my handbag and I could give her some signed blank cheques.'

'You don't give up easily, do you? I tell you what, I'll do a deal with you. If I organize the clothes with Mrs Crichton, will you agree to stay with my mother for a day or two?'

'But I couldn't possibly, she—'

'She would love it and I think you'd like her, too.'

Fiona grinned. 'All right. By the way, any ideas about who pushed that chimney down?'

'I thought I told you to forget about work.'

'Yes, but you won't leave me out of anything, will you?'

'Of course not. The only thing I have in mind at the moment is to see Dr Crichton – I haven't met him yet. I'll give you a ring tomorrow and let you know about any developments. Don't worry, I won't make it too early and spoil your lie-in.'

Noting that the courtyard in front of Crichton's house was empty, Sinclair drove straight in and walked in through the door marked SURGERY.

'My name is Sinclair, Inspector Sinclair,' he said to the receptionist, showing her his warrant card. 'I'm in charge of the Linda Baines case and I believe you've already met my assistant.'

'That's right. Ever such a nice young woman.'

Sinclair nodded. 'Is Dr Crichton in?'

'I'm afraid not. He went up to the hospital to see Miss Pelton a few minutes ago.' The woman looked up at the clock. 'The evening surgery doesn't start for another couple of hours yet, but he'll probably be back before too long if you'd care to wait.'

'Miss Pelton's not seriously ill, I hope.'

'Do you know her, then?'

'Yes, I have met her a couple of times.'

The woman looked round the empty room and then leaned towards him. 'I wouldn't normally tell a soul about it, but seeing as you're a police-officer … she took an overdose yesterday afternoon.'

Sinclair's look of mild concern didn't alter. 'I'm very sorry to hear that. Is she very bad?'

'I don't think so. Dr Crichton told me that all she really needed now was TLC.'

'TLC?'

'Tender loving care.'

'I see. Well, I'm afraid that, as usual, I'm in rather a hurry and as I only want to see Dr Crichton quite briefly, I think I'll go up to the hospital to meet him. Would you be kind enough to give me directions?'

Sinclair was waiting in the front hall of the cottage hospital when Dr Crichton came running down the stairs.

'I just wanted to give you some news of your wife and make my number with you,' Sinclair said, when he had introduced himself.

The man smiled. 'Good of you to come. Why don't we go into the staffroom over there? I know it's empty at the moment.'

Crichton showed the detective in and sat back in one of the armchairs, crossing his legs.

'Nothing's happened to Helen, I hope.'

'No, she's fine.'

'Good. She was in a highly emotional state when she left here and when she gets like that she can drink more than is good for her.'

'We believe that someone quite deliberately tried to

point the finger of suspicion at your wife by breaking the trafficator cover on her Peugeot and leaving the bits at the site of the murder. I'm quite satisfied now that she wasn't responsible for knocking Linda off her bicycle.'

'That's a relief, I must say. I never had any doubt about Helen's innocence myself, but you know what small country towns can be like. It was most upsetting having the finger of suspicion pointed at her.'

'That I can well believe. Does she have enemies here?'

'Any number, I'm afraid. Helen has never really settled into village life and she can be aggressive and rude when she has too much alcohol on board. In many ways, I blame myself for her behaviour.'

'Oh? Why?'

'Like a lot of doctors, I'm afraid I haven't been much of a husband. It's very easy to let the job take over your whole life and then, before you realise what's going on, you've ruined your marriage. It might have been different if we'd had a family, but it just didn't happen despite there being nothing obviously wrong with either of us. The idea of adoption wasn't attractive and may be losing that opportunity was a mistake, too. Anyway, it's too late now.'

'As I said, your wife is perfectly all right, but she was nervous of staying in your brother's flat in view of what happened here and she's moved. I'm sure she'll write or give you a ring soon, but at the moment she doesn't want anyone to know where she is and I have to tell you that that includes you.'

Crichton shook his head sadly. 'I can't say I'm altogether surprised.'

'There was one other thing I wanted to ask you about and that's Miss Pelton.'

PETER CONWAY

'Miss Pelton?'

'Yes. I was wondering if she was well enough to see me. I have met her before, I do know what has happened to her and I'll make it very brief.'

'How did you hear about it?'

'The overdose? You know better than me what places like this are like. There is an important question I want to ask her about Linda and as she liked the girl very much, I think she would want to help.'

Crichton frowned and hesitated before replying. 'Physically, there's no real problem, but the psychological aspects are quite another matter. She refuses to see a psychiatrist and won't tell me why she did it. My guess is that it was more of a cry for help than a genuine suicide attempt; she can only have taken those tablets half an hour or so before she must have known that Miss Pargeter was coming back. Perhaps it's her heart that's been getting to her. It's not that it's that bad, but it takes some people that way – they seem to lose all confidence once they start getting angina. Anyway, I have no doubt that she badly needs to talk to someone and perhaps you'll have more luck than me. I've got some more patients to see and I'll be here for another half-hour or so should you want me. In any case, I'd better come up to the ward with you to clear your visit with sister.'

'Is Miss Pelton in the ward proper?'

'Yes, but in a side room. It has got windows all round it, but it's pretty well sound-proof and you can always draw the curtains.'

The woman was lying with her face to the wall and she didn't move when Sinclair closed the door of the cubicle.

'Miss Pelton, it's Mark Sinclair here. I know about the shepherd-girl – someone sent it round to you, didn't they? You want me to find out who did it and who killed Linda, don't you?' He saw the almost imperceptible shake of her head. 'Roberta didn't murder her, you know.'

Very slowly the frail woman, her face white and strained, turned over in the bed and looked at him.

'Are you quite sure?'

Sinclair wasn't, not by any means, but there was no trace of doubt either in his facial expression or confident tone of voice.

'Absolutely certain. I believe Linda's killer sent you that figurine in order to get the finger of suspicion pointed at Roberta; that's why it's so important for me to find out exactly what happened. It's one of the best leads we have.'

A tear slowly coursed its way down the woman's cheek as she gently nodded her head.

'All right.'

Hesitatingly, she told him about the figurine and the note attached to the shoe-box, but the things she could not bring herself to mention were the photographs of Linda.

'What did you do with the note?'

'I set fire to it and washed the ashes down the sink. I realize now that you're here that it was a stupid thing for me to have done, but I was so devastated by what had happened that I acted without thinking.'

'Tell me as much as you can about it.'

'It was typed on an old machine; I'm quite sure of that and it wasn't very well done, either. It said that the figurine had been found in Sir Geoffrey's summer-house, where Linda used to meet Roberta and that they behaved there "in a blatantly immoral fashion". It also implied that Roberta had not merely found Linda's body, but had killed her beforehand.'

'Where was Roberta that afternoon?'

'She went for a long walk with Louis.'

'At what time did she leave your cottage?'

'It must have been about four-fifteen, directly after we'd had a cup of tea.'

'Are you absolutely certain that the writer of that note used the expression "in a blatantly immoral fashion"?'

'Oh yes. It stuck in my mind. Even though I was so upset, I can remember thinking that it was a pompous way of putting it.'

'What did you do after burning the letter?'

'I put the figurine on the dressing-table so that Roberta would see it, then swallowed all the sleeping tablets in the bottle and lay down on the bed. What the note said made sense; I remembered the looks that Roberta had given Linda, the way she used to put her hand on her shoulder when she thought I wasn't looking and I could understand that she might have killed her if she was being black-mailed. I loved Roberta, I still do, and I didn't want to live after what had happened.'

'I see.'

Sinclair looked at the woman straight in the eye and although he spoke quite softly, he put every ounce of authority he could muster into his voice.

'It's quite clear that Roberta did give Linda that figurine and although I'm equally sure that she was attracted to her and gave in to sexual temptation, she didn't really love her and she most certainly did not kill her. Now, I realize that you were a nurse and probably know more about this than I do, but some people, women as well as men, often those with high drives in other directions, have very powerful sexual impulses, too. For those of us with less powerful urges it is difficult to comprehend why they can't resist them, but I do assure you that they are often quite incapable of doing so, even if it leads them into destructive situations. Linda had a very bad effect on people, not only on Roberta, but on the murderer and others who, one might say, ought equally to have known better. The fact that they may not entirely be able to help what they are doing does not, I realize, make it any easier for those whom they really love and who love them, to accept.' The detective smiled and gave her hand a squeeze. 'Forgive the little lecture, but Linda has caused quite enough misery in the village already and the time has come for it to stop.'

Had it worked? Sinclair wasn't sure, but at least the woman had seemed to be listening and she hadn't clammed up on him.

On the off-chance of finding Atherton in the church the detective tried the door. Finding it unlocked he went inside. When there was no reply to his call he knocked on the half-open door of the vestry. Once again, there was no response. On going in, he saw at once that the vicar must only just have left; the electric kettle and teapot were still hot and the unwashed cup, plate and knife were sitting in the sink.

Sinclair stood there for a moment, wrapped in thought, then decided that there might be advantages in seeing Atherton the following morning rather than hanging about now on the off-chance that the man would come back. In any case, he was due back in Oxford in only a couple of hours for another meeting with Watson. He gave a deep sigh, got into his car, put on a cassette of some Telemann sonatas and drove off to the soothing accompaniment of the baroque music.

'Good morning.'

The man who was unlocking the door of the church whirled round. For a moment, he failed to recognize the detective, then clearly did so, his thin lips coming together in an expression of irritation.

'I'm sorry to disturb you,' Sinclair said, 'but I wonder if we might go back to your house? There have been some developments in the Linda Baines case that I would like to discuss with you.'

'I was just going to …'

'I wouldn't have made a special visit if it hadn't been important.'

'Very well.'

They made their way across to the vicarage and Atherton led the way into his study.

'Don't worry about me if you want to smoke,' Sinclair said, as the man began to fiddle with the cigarette packet on his desk, 'it doesn't bother me in the least.'

Atherton declined the offer, pushing the packet to one side. 'Now,' he said, 'what is it you wanted to say to me?'

'I would like to know what you were doing on the afternoon that Linda Baines was murdered.'

'Inspector, this is preposterous. You interrupt my intended devotions by telling me that there have been developments in the case and then you ask me a stupid question. If you must know, I was reviewing the sermon I had delivered that morning in the light of the congregation's reactions and after that I spent some time relaxing with the Sunday papers.'

'But you also went for a walk, or was it a drive as well?'

'What do you mean?'

'Linda Baines was in the summer-house in Sir Geoffrey's garden that afternoon and had sex with a young man. I think you saw her on the way there and followed her on foot.'

'Don't be absurd, Inspector!'

'You left your "visiting card" near the summer-house. You find smoking a comfort at times of stress, don't you, even in the church – you no doubt remember that first time we met in the vestry. We found two of your cigarette-ends behind a tree within sight and no doubt sound of the summer-house.'

'There are plenty of people who smoke the same brand as me – Belling does, for one, and he was—'

'He was what? There in his garden that afternoon and nearly caught you? You thought that Linda was the personification of evil, didn't you, and that belief was reinforced by the fact that you couldn't get her out of your mind. There was that episode with the boy in the church and there was also her streak at that cricket match a few weeks ago. She tortured you in a way, didn't she, Atherton, with her blatant sexuality – blatant is a word you're rather fond of, isn't it – and was that episode in the summer-house too much for you? You were disturbed by that dog and by Belling as well, but did you wait until Linda left and then go after her in your car?'

'This is outrageous, I ...'

'You don't like Helen Crichton, either, do you? And someone who didn't like her tried to make it look as if she was the guilty one. Not only that, an attempt was made on her life yesterday morning. Would you mind telling me what you were doing then at around ten-thirty?'

'I was at a committee meeting planning events in support of our organ fund, if you must know. Geoffrey Belling will be able to confirm it; he was in the chair.' Atherton suddenly stopped fiddling with the cigarette packet and looked the detective straight in the eye. 'I was in Belling's garden that afternoon, but I didn't kill Linda Baines, I swear it.'

'Tell me exactly what happened.'

'As it was a nice afternoon I decided to walk over to the Hall to deliver the minutes of the previous meeting of the organ-restoration committee; Belling is very particular about them and always likes to check them himself before they are sent out. I went by the back lane as it is a prettier walk and it was then that I saw Linda Baines. She was just coming out of the undergrowth opposite the gate and as I watched she climbed over it and disappeared. I knew she was up to no good, particularly when I found that she had hidden her bicycle there. I found her easily enough – she and that nasty child, Tracey Farrell, were giggling in the summer-house and I decided to wait to see what they were up to. I thought it would probably be nothing more than smoking and drinking, but quite soon Tracey came out and a young man arrived. I hadn't seen that dog of his and I very nearly stepped on it when he came to collect it.'

'And you no doubt heard what went on.'

'It was absolutely disgusting, that girl should have been—'

'You can spare me the outrage bit, Atherton, you don't have to justify yourself to me; all I'm interested in is finding out exactly what happened. I understand that Belling came back that afternoon unexpectedly early; did you see him, by any chance?'

'As a matter of fact I did. I went to look at the summer-house after the boy and the two girls had gone and he was standing in the lane, looking towards the gate.'

'Did he see you?'

'I don't think so.'

'And what did you find in the summer-house?'

'It was locked.'

'Yes, I'm sure it was, but you saw Tracey Farrell put the

key on a hook under the eaves and then you decided to take a look inside a few days later, didn't you? There wasn't much of interest there, was there, apart from that rather attractive piece of Meissen porcelain and a girlie magazine which you also seemed to have found irresistible?' All the colour drained out of the man's face, confirming what Sinclair knew already. 'You're as quick on the uptake as the next man, aren't you, Atherton, and having seen the pair of figurines when you went to tea with Miss Pelton and having heard later that one of them had been broken, you knew at once what had happened, didn't you? It was a golden opportunity to get in a dig at Miss Pargeter, whom you disliked in a way that almost amounted to an obsession, and you grabbed it with both hands, quite literally no doubt. Leaving anonymous notes is a cowardly thing to do and it's only a matter of the greatest good fortune that you haven't Miss Pelton's death on your conscience as well. You look puzzled. Perhaps you hadn't heard that she took an overdose, luckily without serious consequences to her physical well-being, although one couldn't say the same about her psychological distress.'

'I've heard more than enough of this, Inspector, I'm going to—'

'You were careless, Atherton, and one of our men found some fingerprints on the lock of that croquet-box, which matched those on the knife I borrowed from the vestry yesterday and which will be returned to you in due course. If you are charged you may, if you're lucky, get away with being bound over to keep the peace, but even if Miss Pelton decides not to press matters, you may think it prudent to find another living, particularly as you seem to make something of a habit of leaving anonymous notes, not a very desirable characteristic for a vicar in a village like this.'

'What do you mean?'

'Come on. Are you trying to tell me that you didn't throw a brick through the windscreen of Helen Crichton's car with a message wrapped round it? And what about the broken trafficator cover that put suspicion on her in the first place?'

'I don't know what you're talking about.'

'We'll see about that. By the way, you weren't thinking of going anywhere just yet, were you? I'd like another chat with you later.'

As the detective walked towards his car he saw the uniformed constable standing by it.

'Inspector Sinclair?'

'Yes.'

'PC Grimes, sir. DC Campbell has been on the phone and would like you to ring her back urgently on this number. Would you like to come to the station?'

'No thank you, I'll use the car phone.'

Sinclair listened to Fiona in silence while she spoke for several minutes.

'Is he absolutely certain? ... I see. And what about you? Are you quite sure that you're well enough? ... Very well, I'll pick you up at my mother's house at about three – I have something important to attend to first.'

Sinclair drove slowly towards the Hall and stopped at the spot where Linda had been killed, standing there deep in thought for several minutes before continuing on his way.

CHAPTER TWELVE

Geoffrey Belling came out to meet him as Sinclair pulled up in front of the house, the tyres crunching on the gravel.

'Is George Baines here today? I'd rather like a word with him.'

'Yes, he's fussing over my new car at the moment. He only picked it up for me in Reading on Monday and it hardly needs a wash, but at least he's showing an interest in something, which is no bad thing.'

'So you've got rid of the Jaguar, have you?'

'Yes, it was four years old and I was tempted by the new Lexus. It's come just at the right time in one way; I don't like driving long distances and George can get down to some chauffeuring again, which will be good for both of us.'

'Does Baines wear a uniform?'

Belling laughed. 'Only on special occasions, when I'm trying to impress someone. He looks rather good in it, in fact.'

'Do you think I might have a look at the car?'

'Of course. George will be only too happy to show it off in all its glory.'

Belling led the detective to the garage where Baines was working.

'George, you remember Inspector Sinclair, don't you? He'd like another word with you.'

Baines, who was wearing an old green pullover, worn corduroys and Wellington boots, turned off the hose and stared at the detective for a moment.

'Why don't we go into my study?'

'I'll 'ave to go an' change, sir.'

'That won't be necessary,' Sinclair said. 'Why don't you just slip those shoes on and come as you are?'

The detective had little doubt that Belling would have strong views about protocol and he was not surprised to note the fact that the man obviously resented his authority having been usurped, particularly on his own property, but he was too well-mannered to say anything and the slight pursing of his lips was his only sign of displeasure.

'I expect you'd like me to be there, George.'

Belling clearly had no intention of being contradicted by either of them and Sinclair decided to let it rest there. He followed the two men to the house and into the study. The detective doubted if Sir Geoffrey was often nervous, but he was now, Sinclair thought. The man was playing with the paper-weight on his desk and then, when the detective showed no sign of being in any hurry to start, began to beat a gentle tattoo on his knee with his forefinger.

'Mrs Crichton went up to London to stay in her brother-in-law's flat after someone damaged her car on Thursday night and left a threatening note wrapped round a brick. Yesterday morning, a chimney-stack was pushed down from the roof above the flat and two people were injured, one of them quite seriously. Mrs Crichton was clearly the intended victim and whoever the assailant was obviously thought that she was the one who had killed Linda, but not only was he wrong about that – Mrs Crichton has a watertight alibi for the time in question – he also got the wrong person. My assistant, Fiona Campbell, also happened to be in the flat and as it was raining when she left, she borrowed Mrs Crichton's umbrella and was hit by the debris and knocked down into the area.'

'Get to the point, Sinclair. What has that to do with George?'

'On Monday morning, a brand-new, black saloon was parked for some time within sight of the flat and a chauffeur, smartly dressed in a grey uniform, matching cap and very brightly polished brown shoes, gained entry to the house above the basement flat by helping an elderly woman with her shopping-basket. Where did you go, Mr Baines, after you had collected the Lexus from Reading? And perhaps you'd also be good enough to show me the clothes you were wearing on Tuesday morning. The scene-of-crime experts spent a long time up on the roof and found a good deal of evidence there; enough, I believe, to be able to identify the person in question.'

'You don't have to answer, George. Let me get hold of Mr Grimble for you – he'll be the best person to advise you.'

Baines looked from his employer to the detective, who flicked a speck of dust off one leg of his trousers and looked up.

'I take it that Mr Grimble is your solicitor.' Belling nodded. 'Why not ask him to meet us at the Welbury police station and then we can get an agreed statement typed out?'

'It's orl right, sir, I'd like to explain what 'appened.'

'George—'

'I want to, I need to.'

*

After the two detectives had left on the Wednesday after his daughter's murder, George Baines settled into the easy-chair in the bedroom that Sir Geoffrey had provided for him and closed his eyes. His anger at the thought of them poking around Linda's belongings took a long time to settle, but later on, he sank into a cocoon of misery, such that he was quite unaware of the passage of time.

'George! George!'

Baines looked up bemusedly. 'Oh,'ello, Sir Geoffrey.'

'George, go along the corridor, have a bath and a shave and while you do that, I'll make sure that the lodge is properly locked up and get you a change of clothes. After that, you and I must have a talk.'

It was a help, a great help. Baines had never discussed Linda properly with anyone apart from Miss Pembleton and she didn't really count.

'I feel so guilty about 'er, sir.'

'Guilty? Whatever for?'

"Cause I didn't keep proper control of 'er an' if I 'ad 'ave done, none of this would 'ave 'appened.'

'There was nothing wrong with Linda, George, or the way you brought her up. She was just high-spirited, that's all. She would have settled down all right. At one time, you were a bit of a tearaway yourself, if I remember correctly, and look what happened to you. No one could have looked after Rose and Linda better than you did and you've been my right-hand man for more years than I care to remember. Now, there's something I need to talk to you about – the joint funeral. You've been in no shape to discuss it up to now, so I have taken the liberty of making some arrangements for Saturday week, knowing that you might well wish to cancel them. I had the strong feeling that you would want a proper ceremony and yet not one involving gawping onlookers, the attentions of the local press and, dare I say it, even Cyril Atherton. Am I right?'

Baines nodded.

'Well, here's what I suggest. The private chapel here hasn't been used for some time – not since Margot died, in fact – but my cousin Rupert, who officiated on that occasion, has provisionally agreed to hold a service there and I would personally consider it an honour were you to agree to Rose and Linda being buried next to my family. As to those you would like to be present, I leave that entirely to you. Don't give me an answer now; think about it and let me know in due course; there's no hurry, no hurry at all.'

'I don't need to, sir. I can't think of anythin' I'd like better – this was our 'ome.'

Slowly Baines began to lose some of his apathy, doing odd jobs for Sir Geoffrey around the grounds and gradually his appetite began to come back. It was when he was coming down to breakfast on the Saturday, which Mrs Webster, Sir Geoffrey's housekeeper, had been giving him every day in the kitchen, that he heard a voice coming through the half-open door, which he recognized as belonging to Betty Carter, one of the women from the village who came in to do the ironing.

'I'm not surprised she's had to go away – I can't think why the police haven't arrested her. The person I feel sorry for is Dr Charles and it's lucky for her that his brother, Mr Paul, is in America and that his flat in London's free.'

'Arrested? Whatever are you talking about, Betty?'

'Haven't you heard? The police found some glass from Mrs Crichton's car on the road near where Linda was killed.'

'They never!'

'Yes, our Janet's been helping Susan Grimes with her new baby and she overheard Fred talking about it to the garage on the telephone. You'd think she would've had the sense not to get it repaired locally, wouldn't you?'

'Worse for the drink again, I suppose.'

'That's not the half of it. I met Hilda at the WI yesterday and she told me that that woman hadn't been sober for a week.'

'Did she tell you about Mrs Crichton going to London?'

'Indeed she did and couldn't hide her relief, either. Hilda's never accepted her; she's often told me that she couldn't understand why Dr Charles married her in the first place. It wasn't only the drink; do you know ...'

Baines had heard enough. He turned, walked quietly up the stairs and then coughed loudly as he came back down again.

'Good morning, Mr Baines. What do you fancy today?'

'I think I'll 'ave bacon an' egg.'

'Glad to hear your appetite's back, Mr Baines.'

He nodded to the other woman, then picked up the local paper and buried his face in it while the housekeeper busied herself with cooking his breakfast. He got through the meal somehow – he had no wish to have that busy-body Mrs Webster telling Sir Geoffrey that he was still off his food – and then he went back in his room.

It all made sense to him now; the Crichton woman must have killed Linda by knocking her off her bike with her car and then been sufficiently sober to have tried to make it look like a rape. But why, if the police had found the glass on the road, hadn't they arrested her? Baines knew the answer to that one. He hadn't worked for Sir Geoffrey for all those years without knowing what influence people like him and Dr Crichton had locally. But even if Helen

Crichton was going to escape the law, she wasn't going to escape him, by God she wasn't.

It was as if he had suddenly been given a new lease of life. Knowing that Linda hadn't been raped after all somehow made her death easier to bear. There was also someone on whom to focus his anger and hatred. His first priority was to find the woman's address in London and that he achieved with the minimum of difficulty. There were only a few Crichtons in the London telephone directory, even fewer with a 'P' as one of their initials and it was only on the second call that he made from the lodge that he felt a quickening of his pulse as the woman's voice came through on the other end of the line.

'Is Paul there, please?'

'No, I'm afraid he's in America.'

'Sorry to 'ave troubled you.'

Baines couldn't have said that he recognized the voice, but it was certainly slurred, the woman hadn't queried the Christian name and she had mentioned America. It was plenty enough for him. When he got back to the Hall, he took the London A-Z out of the glove-pocket of the Lexus and looked up the address. Maida Vale wasn't a part of the capital he knew, but at least it was within walking distance of Paddington station, which was the terminus from Reading.

Baines went up to London by the afternoon train. After leaving Paddington he walked up Edgware Road and after about a mile turned left into Elgin Avenue. The flat was in the basement of a house in the middle of a long terrace in a broad street less than ten minutes on foot from Maida Vale underground station. He walked along the pavement and stopped right outside it, pretending to be doing up his shoe laces.

Unlike many of the other houses, the steps leading down to the area were clean and free from litter, but the front windows, barred like the others in the neighbouring basements, were so dirty as to be almost opaque. Baines spent a good hour wandering up and down the road and in that time, the only person who went into the part of the house above the basement flat was an elderly woman with a shopping basket on wheels, who had considerable difficulty in negotiating the stone steps and unlocking the front door.

It was obvious that the whole street was undergoing a steady process of renovation and upgrading; several of the houses, each of which consisted of four floors and a basement, had been refaced and repainted in the recent past and had also been fitted with new window-frames. Looking through into the front rooms, he could also see that the carpets and many of the furnishings were of the highest quality. The house some six doors along the road had scaffolding up its whole height and there was a gang of men working on both the interior and exterior. In contrast to the others, the building in which he was interested was one of the most dilapidated. The plaster was badly cracked and discoloured, most of the wood of the window-sills was rotten, with the paint flaking off, and one of the upper windows was broken, the glass having been replaced by a rectangle of plywood.

What to do next? Baines thought long and hard about it on his way back to Reading on the train and by the time he had taken the bus back to Welbury and walked to the Hall, he had it all worked out. As a start, what he really wanted to do was to see Mrs Crichton to make absolutely certain that she was there and whether she was in the flat alone. He also wanted to know if the police were keeping a watch on her.

One problem was that the flat was such a difficult place to keep under observation; he would be far too conspicuous hanging about for any length of time in such an open street and there wasn't a convenient café, or anywhere else from which he could watch it. The Jaguar would, in some ways, be the best answer to that. He was quite sure that if he asked in the right way Sir Geoffrey would lend it to him, and if he put on his chauffeur's uniform no one would pay any attention to him however long he sat in it. It was true that the street was in a restricted-parking area, with only a very few meters, most of the bays being for residents, but if he kept an eye open for traffic wardens, that shouldn't present any problems, either. The one snag was that after their row following their near-miss in Welbury, Mrs Crichton would almost certainly recognize the car, particularly with its distinctive maroon colour.

On the Saturday morning Baines was still wondering what to do, when Sir Geoffrey sent for him.

'You know that Lexus I've had on order for some time? Well, I've just had a call from the garage in Reading to say that it'll be ready to pick up on Monday. Would you be kind enough to do that for me?'

'Be glad to, sir. Would you mind if I went for a bit of a run in it afterwards? I'd like to make myself thoroughly familiar with it before taking you out.'

'Good idea. You'll be able to show me all the odds and ends when you get back.'

On the Monday morning Baines drove the Jaguar out of the garage, stopped at the lodge to change into his chauffeur's uniform and was at the dealer in Reading by nine. Even though he was impatient to be on his way, he listened carefully to what the salesman had to say and it was 9.45 before he was able to leave. Normally he was a relaxed driver, but the responsibility of a brand-new and such an expensive car and the stress of the London traffic made him tense and anxious. For once he was relieved when the journey was over and he was parked within sight of the flat in Maida Vale.

At that hour of the morning, the street was very quiet; those with jobs had clearly gone off to work and that left the shoppers, a few visits from delivery vans and the men on the building-site. It had started to drizzle and half an hour later he was sitting in the car, keeping an eye out for traffic wardens, when he saw movement from the basement flat and Mrs Crichton appeared, opening a large, multicoloured golfing umbrella when she reached the top of the steps.

Being a keen birdwatcher, Sir Geoffrey always kept a pair of binoculars in his car, which Baines had transferred when he had left the Jaguar in Reading. He took them out of their case, focusing them on the woman. He wasn't able to see much apart from the fact that she was carrying a shopping-basket and he watched her out of sight round the corner. Not long after, he caught sight of the old woman he had seen previously, slowly approaching from the direction of the local shops. He decided at once that the opportunity was too good to miss.

'May I help you, madam?'

Her sudden look of alarm was replaced by a smile when she saw the way he was dressed and the gleaming new car on the other side of the road.

'That would be kind. I've got rather a heavy load this morning and the steps are a bit awkward.'

He did everything slowly and carefully so as not to cause her any anxiety, lifting her basket to the top of the steps and then standing respectfully to one side as she unlocked the door. He held it open for her, touched his cap briefly when she thanked him and, as she walked across the lobby towards her front door on the ground floor, he went outside, allowing the door to come back towards him on its spring. He checked it at the end of its travel so that the lock wouldn't engage. Looking around, he saw that there was no one about and, after waiting until he heard no further sounds from the old woman, he pushed the door open again and ran up the stairs.

There was a carpet, although it wasn't much of one, being threadbare in places and very dirty, but it did serve to deaden his footsteps and he climbed noiselessly right to the top. Each landing was lit by a small window, which gave a view of the street, with the exception of the one at the top of the house where there was a skylight. There was a length of thick cord hanging from a ratchet at one side of it, but the mechanism was rusty and it was obvious from the mixture of accumulated dirt and cobwebs that it hadn't been opened for years.

Back in the street, just before getting into the car again, he looked up at the roof and saw immediately that if only he could gain access to it, it might be the answer he was looking for. There were two tall chimney-stacks behind which he could conceal himself and the area between them was flat and protected by a low brick balustrade, which ran the length of the terrace. Baines picked up the binoculars and spent ten minutes scanning the roofs with even greater care. Ever since he had first looked at the roofs he had had an idea about how he might achieve his aim. The tall chimney-stack directly above the entrance to the basement was even more weathered than the balustrade, with crumbling brick showing through the areas where the plaster had come away. He was convinced that if he did some preliminary work one good push would bring the whole thing down. He needed further time for thought though, and, deciding not to wait for Helen Crichton's return, he drove back to Welbury.

Sir Geoffrey was full of enthusiasm for the new car and Baines spent the afternoon with him, going over the hand-book, showing him where everything was and then accompanying him when he took it out for a run.

'I'm feeling' much more me old self, sir,' he said, when they got back, 'and although I've very much appreciated your kind offer of the bed 'ere, I think it's time for me to go back to the lodge. There are Linda's and Rose's things to sort aht and if I don't do it now, I know I'll never get rahnd to it.'

'You're probably right, but if it doesn't work out, you will let me know, won't you?'

'Yes, I will, sir.'

'What about your evening meal tonight?'

'I thought I'd treat meself to one at a pub in Reading; I know the landlord a bit.'

'Good idea.'

That night Baines took the last train to Paddington after having had a substantial meal in Reading. When he arrived he walked the mile and a half from the station to Maida Vale. He had on his rubber-soled walking-boots, his thickest trousers, two heavy sweaters and an anorak. Inside a hold-all were his own binoculars, a torch, a hammer and chisel, a thin pair of gloves in addition to the thick ones he was wearing, and several bars of chocolate and some apples.

Largely, he imagined, because they were still at the stage of doing the internal demolition work on the house along the road – even the window-frames had been taken out – no attempt had been made to guard it or the scaffolding and it was the work of a moment to slip through the hole where the front window had been. He waited inside for a minute or two to make sure that no one was going to raise the alarm; then, shading his torch with his hand, he crept out into the hall. Access to the roof was as easy as he had hoped; there was also scaffolding at the back of the house and all he had to do was climb the staircase, go outside on the top floor and then pull himself up.

The roofs were all connected, merely being separated by low brick walls. Ten minutes after leaving the street he was looking down through the skylight, which he had already seen from the inside. It was too dark to inspect the chimney-stack properly and he pulled on his Balaclava helmet, lay down and made himself as comfortable as he could with his head resting on the hold-all. To his surprise he slept quite well and it was already beginning to get light by the time he woke up. After eating one of the apples he had a careful look round with the binoculars.

One or two early commuters were walking along the street below, but otherwise all was quiet. He couldn't see Mrs Crichton going out much before ten and if that proved to be the case he would have a good three to four hours in which to work on the chimney. Not, he thought, that it was likely to require as long as that. When he gave its side a push, he felt it give slightly and he had no doubt that it would fall over in that direction easily enough but getting it to go over the balustrade clearly wouldn't prove nearly so simple.

He was anxious to finish the job as quickly as possible, but before beginning, decided to see if he could find an alternative escape route, as even though he was out of sight of the men working on the house at the end of the row, he clearly would be unable to get back to the street that way. Going through one of the other skylights, which were fitted to all the houses, was an obvious possibility and he found one near the end of the row which looked promising.

The wood of its frame was rotten and it was secured by a long, hinged, metal bar, which was perforated by a series of holes which fitted into a metal stud set into the surround. The wood was so soft that he was able to pull large pieces of it away and, by using his chisel to finish the job, he managed to push the metal bar free and lift the skylight up. After he had cleared the pieces of wood away he jammed it open by using a piece of the chimney-pot which had fallen off one of the nearby stacks. Then he returned to his previous position and set to work on the brickwork. By nine o'clock he had loosened the mortar all around the base with his chisel and chipped enough of the lower bricks away at the end furthest from the street to give himself a good handhold. When he was finally satisfied he collected up the pieces of brick and mortar, put them into the plastic bag he had brought for the purpose and ate the food he had brought with him.

It was soon after ten when he heard the distant rumble of thunder. Looking over to the west he saw the dark clouds building up. Suppose, he thought, it settled in to rain steadily and Helen Crichton failed to come out all day? What would he do then? The chimney was now unsafe and he couldn't leave it there to fall on some innocent passer-by. Perhaps it hadn't been such a wonderful idea after all and the safest thing would be to stay there all day and then push it down during the night when no one was about.

He took a cautious look over the balustrade when he felt

the first few drops of heavy rain. He was just stepping back when he heard a door below slam. Leaning over again, he saw the multicoloured umbrella just going up. Baines moved swiftly to the back of the chimney-stack, squatted down like a weightlifter, took a grip on the edge of the cavity where he had chiselled the bricks away and pulled up with all his strength. Just as the chimney began to topple over, destroying the balustrade as it fell into the street, there was a brilliant flash of lightning, which was so close that he heard it sizzle, followed almost immediately by a deafening crack of thunder almost directly overhead.

Pausing just to pick up his hold-all and with the rain beating down on his shoulders, Baines made his way across the roofs towards the skylight which he had left propped open. It took him only a few moments to get inside and climb down. After he had closed it fully he ran down the three flights of stairs, stopping short of the hall when he saw a young Indian woman, who had clearly come from the ground-floor flat and was looking out of the open front door.

Anxious though he was to get away, he decided not to risk being seen and waited just out of sight. After about ten minutes he heard the siren and, reflected in the mirror above the table in the hall, the flashing blue light of an ambulance. It was not until it had left that the Indian woman went back into her flat and he was able to get out on to the street. The worst of the rain had by now subsided and no one paid him any attention as he walked along the pavement. He saw that the chimney had fallen half on to the pavement and half into the area. He went up to an elderly man who was one of a group of people which was now beginning to disperse.

'What happened?'

'Lightning brought down the chimney-stack.'

'Anybody hurt?'

'Dead as mutton, someone was saying. Young woman underneath. Never had a chance.'

'Did you see it yourself?'

'No. Heard the crash and came out when the rain stopped. Bloody great flash of lightning there was and then the thunder; that and the chimney coming down frightened the life out of my old moggy, I can tell you.'

Baines was wet through, but hardly noticed it as he sat in the train on the way back to Reading. Linda had been avenged, cleanly and efficiently and everyone would think that it was an act of God. In a way it was, he thought; there had been something biblical about that flash of lightning coming at that particular moment; it was almost as if he had been God's instrument of justice.

After he had left the police station in Welbury where George Baines had signed his statement, Sinclair drove back to his mother's house. What an unholy mess this case was, he thought. Would Baines get over the whole business in time? It would, he thought, very much depend on what sort of sentence he got and on Belling, who would presumably put up bail for him and pay for a top barrister. With that and a good psychiatrist, it wasn't beyond the bounds of possibility that the man might even get away with a suspended sentence in view of all the circumstances. Certainly, Belling could hardly have been more concerned about George Baines' welfare that afternoon, but was that just the act of a good and conscientious employer or was it the result of guilt about Linda? Was it just chance that the man had been near the summer-house on that Sunday afternoon, or had he, too, been seduced by the girl's fatal attraction? Sinclair just didn't know and he was by no means sure that he wanted to find out. And what about all the other sad casualties? One thing was clear and that was that it was going take a very long time for all those who lived in Welbury to get over it.

CHAPTER THIRTEEN

With the help of a couple of pain-killing tablets and the sleeping-pill that she had been given, Fiona had a surprisingly good night, but the same could certainly not have been said about the following morning. She tried to sit up when Mrs Sinclair came in to see how she was and was quite incapable of effective movement.

'Poor old you, you are in a bad way,' the woman said.

Fiona had never been so stiff in her life before; her neck, back and limbs felt as if they were encased in plaster and even the attempt at turning on to her side was so painful that it forced an involuntary groan out of her.

Mrs Sinclair shook her head. 'I really think that you should—'

'You're not going to send me back to hospital, are you?'

The woman laughed. 'What have you got against hospitals? Mark was telling me how you practically fought to get out yesterday. No, I was just thinking that a hot bath might be the best thing for you – that was just about the only way my husband was able to get his joints loose once the arthritis got so bad – but we also have to think about that graze on your back, don't we? Why don't I take a look at it? I'm no sort of nurse, but Tony developed a pressure sore after his stroke and I became quite expert at dealing with that.'

She rolled Fiona on to her side and very gently eased her nightdress up.

'My goodness, you did take a battering! How's that?'

'Painful!'

'I'm afraid the dressing's badly stuck. What do you think? Shall we leave it, or try to soak it off?'

'I've just got to have that bath.'

If anyone had told Fiona a couple of days earlier that she would be given a shower on one day and a bath on the next, she would have laughed them to scorn. She had always been shy about her body, but at least, she thought, she had been cured of that now.

In their different ways, the two women had both helped, Helen Crichton, who had said: 'there's nothing for you to worry about, you've got a very nice bod and I've seen a few in my time, I can tell you,' and Judith Sinclair, who was motherly and comforting. Once the dressing had been soaked off and the intense stinging sensation from the water had worn off, Fiona was able to lie back with her head resting on the bath-pillow and sip the cup of tea that was brought to her.

'I've never been so pampered in my life,' she said half an hour later, when she was eating breakfast, sitting comfortably in an armchair in the living-room.

'Then it's high time you were. I don't know what Mark's up to getting you into such a mess.'

'It was nothing to do with him; he's been ever so nice to me. This is the first time since I started with the police that I've been allowed to take any initiative on my own and it's been great.'

'You sound just like my daughter, Jane. She's a solicitor

and her job's everything to her. What with her and Jenny, who's got the wanderlust, not to mention Mark, I doubt if I'll ever get to be a grandmother.' The woman gave a smile. 'Times have changed, as Jane never stops telling me, and I mustn't become a pathetic old fossil. As long as they're all happy with what they're doing, that's the most important thing.' Mrs Sinclair half rose from her chair. 'Can I get you anything else? Some more toast? Another cup of coffee?'

'No, thank you.'

The woman sat with her until she had finished and then picked up the tray.

'Now, no slacking,' she said briskly. 'Once I've dealt with this, I'll help you to get dressed and then we'll take a turn round the garden.'

Judith Sinclair's no-nonsense approach was just what she had needed, Fiona thought, as she was having a rest in the conservatory before lunch. She had had no time to think about her close call or to feel sorry for herself, and the gentle exercise had helped to ease the stiffness. A few minutes later the phone rang and Mrs Sinclair came in with a cordless phone.

'It's Mark. He's ringing to find out how you are and to give you some news. Lunch is just about ready, but I expect you'd like to have a word with him right away.'

Fiona nodded and sat up. When he had asked her how she was and she had reassured him that she was fine, Sinclair told her about his visit to Amelia Pelton at the hospital.

'Have you got anywhere with that chimney business yet?'

'Yes. I didn't want to worry you with it yesterday, but I'm quite sure that Baines was responsible.' He explained about the findings on the roof and what the woman in the ground-floor flat had said. 'I'm going to see him tomorrow, not a task I'm looking forward to.'

'I can well imagine that. Couldn't I come with you?'

'I'm quite sure you already know the answer to that.'

'But there's nothing really wrong with me – I'm just a bit stiff, that's all.'

'I promise I'll come over tomorrow afternoon and I'll tell you how it went. Has mother been behaving herself?'

'She's been marvellous, absolutely wonderful.'

'I thought you'd like her.'

After lunch Fiona had just dropped off to sleep when Mrs Sinclair came in again.

'Sorry to disturb you again, but it's Mark's secretary. I told her you weren't well, but she said it was extremely urgent and that she must speak to you.'

The woman didn't waste time on apologies. 'I've just had Dr Rawlings on the line and he wants to see you urgently. I did try to explain that you weren't well, but you know what he's like. I offered to send someone else, but he said firmly that no one else would do, not even Inspector Sinclair.'

'Does Inspector Sinclair know about this call?'

'No. He's not been answering his car phone.'

'May I have Dr Rawlings's number, please?'

'Of course, but I'm afraid that ringing him won't do any good – he was most insistent that you should be the one to go to his laboratory in person and as soon as possible.'

'All right, I'll get there somehow.'

To Fiona's surprise, Judith Sinclair didn't raise any objections and even entered into the spirit of it by providing her with a crêpe bandage in lieu of the bra that she was unable to wear on account of the graze on her back.

'There you are,' she said in triumph. 'Proper nineteen-twenties look without so much as a hint of a wobble to obstruct you in the execution of your duty!'

Judith Sinclair drove confidently into a parking-slot in an area marked 'Consultants Only' after Fiona's warrant card had worked miracles with the attendant at the barrier.

Rawlings took one look at her face when Miss Ryle showed her into his office and held up his hand.

'My dear young lady, I was told that you were unwell, but not that you had been run over by a bus.'

He shook his head when she had explained what had happened.

'No wonder that Sinclair's secretary was trying to protect you. Good of you to have come here, and it won't prove a wasted visit, that I can promise you. When we were discussing the motile sperm in the girl's body and the seminal stains on her underwear, DNA testing had not been completed. When it had, it became clear that they came from two different sources, proving that the girl had had intercourse with two different men within a matter of hours and, what's more, the specimens matched the two separate lots of hair you so providentially provided.'

'Do you mean to say that the results were not the same?'

'I can see that having a chimney land on the top of your head hasn't dulled your wits. Not only were the two sets of DNA quite distinct, but they also matched the two separate lots of hair you so providentially provided.'

'What?'

'I thought that might make you sit up.'

'Which was which?'

'Those you labelled as specimen "A" matched the stains on the girl's panties and "B" the others. Tell me, how did you come by them?' Rawlings nodded when she had explained. 'Yes, that certainly does put the cat amongst the pigeons.'

'Do you think I might try to get Inspector Sinclair on the phone?'

'Miss Ryle will do that for you if you tell her what number to ring. Why don't you lie down while we're waiting – there's a couch through there.'

'No, I'm fine, thank you.'

'You certainly don't look it – you ought to be in hospital.'

'I've got to see this through; it matters to me a great deal.'

'I suppose you want to be in at the denouement.'

'Yes, I do.'

'I admire your spirit, if not your common sense. All right, I won't tell your revered boss that you look like death warmed up and can hardly move, but don't blame me if he jumps to the same conclusion once he sees you.'

Mark Sinclair drove straight into the courtyard of Charles Crichton's house and helped Fiona out of the passenger seat. It was no easy task; she had stiffened badly during the journey down and nearly five minutes went by before she was able to straighten completely.

'Hello,' said the receptionist when they went in. 'I'm afraid the doctor's up at the hospital again. You don't have much luck, do you?'

'I wonder if you'd be good enough to give him a ring? I'd like to have a word with him on the phone.'

The tension which Fiona was feeling intensely didn't appear to have affected Sinclair, who was leaning nonchalantly against the counter. As she watched he was passed the receiver.

'Yes, Sinclair here. I've got some further news about your wife ... I'd rather wait until you get here ... Yes, we are ... Right, thank you.' The detective smiled at the receptionist. 'He's asked us to wait in the house. Don't disturb yourself, my assistant knows the way.'

Fiona did her best to sit still while they were waiting, but she was quite unable to get into a comfortable position. She glanced across at Sinclair to see if her constant fidgeting was irritating him, but he seemed quite oblivious to his surroundings; with his hand on his chin he was deep in thought. Some fifteen minutes later, just when she was thinking that she would have to get up and walk around, Crichton came hurrying in.

'Sorry to have kept you,' he said, holding out his hand to Sinclair. 'I was talking to the relatives of someone who has just died and I couldn't cut it short. You said you wanted to tell me something about Helen; nothing serious, I hope.' He suddenly seemed to notice Fiona's face. 'My dear Miss Campbell, that's a nasty graze you have there. Had an accident?'

'That's part of what I wanted to see you about,' Sinclair said.

'I don't understand.'

'I was a little economical with the truth yesterday; the real reason for your wife leaving your brother's flat was that someone tried to kill her on Tuesday morning by pushing a chimney, which was already in an unsafe condition, down on top of her. Fortunately for her Miss Campbell, who had been visiting her and had borrowed her umbrella, was mistaken for her and was on the receiving end of it instead. She's very lucky to be alive.'

'But who would want to kill Helen?'

'George Baines for one, because he not unreasonably thought she had been responsible for Linda's death. You had had enough of Helen, hadn't you, Dr Crichton, and a manslaughter conviction would have disposed of her nicely.'

'I don't know what you mean?'

'I think you do. I hardly imagine that you aren't familiar with DNA testing and the way it has revolutionized the investigation of rape cases. We heard this morning that the DNA from the seminal specimen from inside Linda's body matched that of your hair. Dr Crichton, I am arresting you on suspicion of having been responsible for the death of Linda Baines. You are not obliged to say anything unless you wish to do so, but ...'

Charles Crichton hardly seemed to be listening to the words of the caution and was looking over the detective's shoulder out of the window, then quite suddenly all the tension went out of his muscles and he sat down heavily, his face pallid and beads of sweat standing out on his forehead.

'I must make arrangements with my receptionist, my patients—'

'I'm afraid that won't be possible; I'm sure she'll cope very well on her own.'

Crichton got to his feet, fists clenched and face flushed, then his shoulders slumped as he saw the powerful figure of Sergeant Stringer, who had appeared at the door.

'Why not come with me, sir? Fred has got the car outside.'

*

A little over two hours later Crichton faced the two detectives across the table in the police station in Welbury and the first interview was taped. The man spoke quietly and fluently with complete lack of emotion and throughout needed very little prompting; it was almost as if he had rehearsed what he was going to say.

'Yes,' he began, 'I killed Linda Baines and I'd like to explain why I did it. Looking back at it all, I can hardly believe that I was the one to have delivered Linda fifteen years ago in the cottage hospital here and that that seven-and-a-half-pound mite should have become the destructive temptress she was.'

'When did it start?'

'The first time I became aware of her in that way was when I was doing the medicals at the school. She took her top things off and when the PE teacher was making a note on her card, Linda gave me a look. I can't begin to describe it, or what exactly made the message so clear, but clear it was. "I know you're interested and I'm available" is what it said. It didn't happen right away, but she started to come to the surgery for trivial complaints and each time, the little smiles, the looks and the body language made it only too clear that I hadn't been mistaken that first time.

'I shall never forget the day it happened. It was no accident that she should have come up to the house one Sunday when both Helen and Hilda were out. She rang the bell and when I answered the door, there she was, doubled up and groaning.

'"I've got a terrible stomach-ache," she said. Did I know what she was up to? I can't really answer that, but what I did was help her into the examination room in the surgery and told her to get on to the couch for me to take a look at her. I left her to slip her things down and when I came back, there she was without a stitch on, sitting cross-legged on the couch and smiling at me.

"You want to, I want to and you've no need to worry, I've done it before and I'm on the pill."

'She was so beautiful, that girl, quite perfectly formed, but she was much more than that; she had a quite incredible sexual presence, like nothing I had ever experienced before. Why, might you ask, was a middle-aged doctor having sex with an under-age girl, who was also one of his patients? I'm not trying to make excuses, just offering an explanation, when I say that it was partly due to the wreckage of my marriage; Helen had become a drunken slut, whom I could hardly bear to look at, let alone touch, there was intense sexual frustration – that side of life had always meant a lot to me – and the fact that Linda, the most sexually attractive girl that I had ever met, wanted me in that way.'

'What do you think her motive was?'

'God alone knows. It's true that I did give her money and presents, but I'm sure it wasn't that – she never made any threats or demands. May be she was telling the truth when she told me that sex was something that she enjoyed more than anything else and that a doctor was the ideal person from whom she would be able to learn all the variations. Does that sound far-fetched to you? It did and does to me, too, but I can't think of any better explanation. What went wrong? Well, I was expecting her that Sunday afternoon and, most unlike her, she was late. She came into the house and, just like that, told me that it was all over because she'd found a young man of her own age.

'If I'd had the sense to wish her luck and thank her for

the good times we'd had together, all would have been well, but I didn't. I was devastated; I pleaded with her, I shouted at her and I told her that she was an ungrateful bitch. Linda wasn't the sort to sit down under something like that. She countered by informing me that I was too old, flabby, not half the young fellow, Phil Rouse, whom she had just left, was and that I was pathetic, whining like a small boy deprived of a packet of sweets.

'I can't explain how I could possibly have reacted in the way I did. If I had hit her in the heat of the moment it might have been understandable, but what I can't comprehend is how I could have been so calculated about what I did do. I followed her bicycle at a distance in the Volvo and when she was out of sight of the village and well on her way home I came up behind her and quite deliberately ran her off the road.

'She was sitting in the undergrowth, holding her leg and crying, and when I came up to her she began to scream. She was making the most terrible noise and without thinking, I picked up a large stone and hit her on the head with it. I dragged her a few yards into a clearing in the trees and then I ... '

'Why did you do that on top of everything else?'

'Why does anyone give in to animal and homicidal impulses? Lust, jealousy and anger at the way she had mocked me? A fatal character flaw? Possession by the devil?'

'What did you do next?'

'When I came to myself, I saw Linda lying there spread-eagled and realized at once that she was dead; I was utterly appalled by what I had done and sat on a tree-stump, not caring whether anyone found my car, her bicycle or me by the side of her body'

'How long where you there?'

'I don't know the answer to that, either, but the instinct for self-preservation must have taken over and when I did act, I did so quite calmly and efficiently. I put on my gloves from the car, pulled the bicycle off the road and then drove home, believing that when Linda was found it would be assumed that she had been attacked and raped by a sex maniac.

'It was the sight of Helen's car in the shed by the side of the house that gave me the idea that this might be the ideal way of dealing with her. I knew what she used to do on Sunday afternoons; I followed her once and found her at it with Earnshaw – he's one of the local farmers – and I was quite sure that the man, being married and with children, would never give her an alibi. As for old Cosgrove, her father, he might just possibly have accepted adultery, but manslaughter would be quite another matter. Why did I care what Cosgrove thought or did? It's because I'm hope-lessly in hock to him. Owning and running an ocean-going yacht costs a small fortune and Cosgrove footed the bill by making interest-free loans, which he made quite clear need not be paid back provided nothing went wrong with our marriage. The agreement, unwritten, of course, and made when he sensed that we were having problems, was that if I stayed with Helen and she stayed with me, the loans would be paid off when he died and the interest from the residue of the estate left to us in trust so long as we remained married.'

'That was a very strange arrangement, wasn't it?'

'Well, Cosgrove is not only a sports fanatic, he also has a thing about marriage for life and also morality in general. I was certain that the combination of drink, adul-tery and finally manslaughter would be the end of it as far as Helen was concerned, and it was my chance to get rid of her. He likes me, does Cosgrove, but he also likes the reflected glory of the races I've won and I had no reason to believe that he would ditch me as well. I broke the plastic cover of the near-side trafficator of Helen's car, walked back through the woods and left the pieces on the road where I'd knocked Linda off her bicycle. When I had replaced the stone in its original position to make it look as if Linda had hit her head on it when she fell off, I had just started to bend down with the intention of adjusting Linda's clothes and altering her position so that it would look as if Helen had dragged her away from the road, when I heard someone approaching through the trees. I only just had time to hide behind a large oak before I saw Miss Pargeter come striding along a path towards the clearing with her dog. Just before I crept away, I remember thinking that even with Linda being found with her clothing disarranged and her legs splayed, it was still possible that once the police found the bits from the trafficator cover of the Peugeot on the road, they might think that Helen had made a deliberate attempt to make it look like a rape. After all, she was both a doctor's wife and had been a physiotherapist and would have had enough knowledge to carry that out. In any case, I had no reason to believe that any suspicion would fall on me.'

'How were you able to face George Baines and carry on with your patients as if nothing had happened?'

'Total denial to myself, I suppose, and the fact that I had almost come to believe that Helen had really done it. That proved to be so much the case that I couldn't bear her presence in the house any longer, particularly as she was drinking more than ever. I couldn't understand why she hadn't been arrested and I decided both to scare the living daylights out of her and give you people a nudge as well.

'She had conveniently left her car in the courtyard overnight as she was so drunk; she didn't hear me break the windscreen during the night and I was able to make sure that she discovered the damage herself by asking her to move the Peugeot first thing on that Friday morning. As I expected, she went completely to pieces and jumped at the suggestion that she might go to my brother's flat in London. I was just waiting for her to be arrested and that's what I thought you had come to tell me this morning.

'I hadn't switched off so completely that the probability of DNA testing didn't occur to me. I assumed that the obvious stains on Linda's underwear would be the focus of attention and if the crunch came it would have been perfectly possible to have started rumours about Phil Rouse. I was confident, too, that if a specimen had also been taken from inside Linda's body and the forensic people went as far as to test some, or even all the males in the village, including myself, I would either be able to evade it, or substitute material from a patient out of the area. Tell me,' he said, 'why was it that you suspected me and had my hair analysed?' He looked straight at Fiona. 'It was you, wasn't it?'

She glanced at Sinclair, who almost imperceptibly shook his head.

'Never mind, it doesn't make any difference.'

'How on earth did you get hold of some of his hair and what made you suspect him' Sinclair asked, when the man had been taken out of the interview room.

'It was just luck, really,' Fiona replied. 'After I left the summer-house where I had picked those hairs off Rouse's sweater, I drove past Crichton's house and saw the broken windscreen of Helen's car in the courtyard. I stopped to ask Crichton about it and afterwards asked him if I could use his phone to ring Rawlings. It was Crichton's own suggestion that it would be more private for me in the house and it was pure nosiness that led me to nip up the stairs and have a snoop around the bedrooms. The sight of Crichton's hairbrush gave me the idea of testing Rawlings a bit by giving him two different lots of hair instead of one to play with and the rest you know. At the back of my mind, too, was the fact that Helen Crichton had originally told me that her husband was having sex with Linda. Although, to be honest, I didn't believe her at the time and you'll remember that she later on said that she had made it up out of spite, I did have some niggling doubts about it and it seemed a good idea to put it to the test, particularly as we hadn't ruled him out as a suspect.'

'That was excellent work and let's have no more talk of luck; you obviously have an instinct for this sort of work and, what's more, the courage to act on it. Thanks to you, Crichton's arrest will be a relief to many people, not least Miss Pelton.'

'Do you think those two will be able to make it up?'

'Who knows, but I would like to see how she is getting on and at least I'll be able to tell her that we've made an arrest, even if I don't give her the details.'

Sinclair put a restraining hand on Fiona's arm as they reached the door of the ward and she saw the strong profile of Miss Pargeter through the window of the cubicle. The woman was sitting by the side of the bed, holding the hand of the slight figure lying against the pillows and as they watched, she bent forward and kissed her friend gently.

'Do you know,' Sinclair said, his voice little more than a whisper, 'people may make private and not so private jokes about people like Miss Pelton and Miss Pargeter, but they have love, they have strong emotions and they have passion; I don't think they're funny at all; in fact, I envy them.'